interrupted

Rachel Cu
Galatians 6:14

interrupted

A life beyond words

Rachel Coker

ZONDERVAN

ZONDERVAN.com/
AUTHORTRACKER
follow your favorite authors

ZONDERVAN

Interrupted
Copyright © 2012 by Rachel Coker

Requests for information should be addressed to:
Zondervan, *Grand Rapids, Michigan* 49530

ISBN 978-0-310-72973-0

All Scripture quotations, unless otherwise indicated, are taken from the King James Version of the Bible.

Any Internet addresses (websites, blogs, etc.) and telephone numbers in this book are offered as a resource. They are not intended in any way to be or imply an endorsement by Zondervan, nor does Zondervan vouch for the content of these sites and numbers for the life of this book.

Cover design: *Gayle Raymer*
Cover photography: *Synergy Photographic*
Interior design: *Greg Johnson, Textbook Perfect*

Printed in the United States of America

12 13 14 15 16 /DCI/ 22 21 20 19 18 17 16 15 14 13 12 11 10 9 8 7 6 5 4 3 2 1

Part One

1939

Chapter 1

A chilly Peace infests the Grass
The Sun respectful lies —
Not any Trance of industry
These shadows scrutinize.

—Emily Dickinson

I stared at the ceiling in silence. Although it was so dark I don't think it could really be called staring at all. More like tilting my chin up in that direction.

My room was cold and quiet, the moon casting eerie shadows through my window over the things that, at thirteen years old, I held dear. My china doll, my stuffed bears, my book collection . . .

"Alcyone," a voice whispered.

I gasped and jerked my head toward the door.

Mama stood by my bed, clad in a milky-white nightgown, her long, dark hair falling down her shoulders. She held a finger up to her lips.

"Come on, Allie," she whispered, grabbing my wrist gently. "I want you to see the stars."

My heart still thumping, I followed her down the hallway, my bare feet pattering on the cold wooden floor. The moon shone on the clock by the staircase. 2:52.

I rubbed my eyes groggily. "Where are we—"

Mama halted in the doorway of the kitchen, the moonlight illuminating her from the back.

"Close your eyes."

I did, and let her lead me out the little door until I could feel the damp grass between my toes. I shivered at everything I could feel and sense: the chilly air, the chirping crickets, the dewy earth ...

"Open them," Mama commanded, lowering her hold from my wrist to my hand.

I did, and the first thing I saw was heaven, the way it was meant to look from earth.

Millions of dazzling stars were strung across the sky above us. Twinkling and dancing and *singing*. My heart skipped a beat.

I knelt on the ground beside Mama and stretched back to see as much of the sky as possible. It just seemed to go on and on, covering the fields around us with a sweet and heavy blanket.

I tilted my head and racked my brain for words to describe it. *Eerie ... dreamy ... alluring ... enthralling ... breathtaking.*

"The moon is distant from the sea," Mama murmured, "and yet with amber hands, she leads him, docile as a boy, along appointed sands."

I turned to look at Mama. She was staring at the sky, a strange look on her face. She was so beautiful ... so light and delicate.

I was confused. "Mama," I whispered, "we aren't at the sea." I'd never been to the sea, and I was quite sure she hadn't been in many, many years.

Mama's lips upturned in a little smile. "That was Dickinson."

She reached over and stroked my cheek. Her eyes had a far-off mist. "One day you'll understand, Allie. One day you'll be a great writer too."

"Is that what you want of me?" I whispered.

Mama nodded slowly, stroking my cheek. "Yes, my miracle. I want you to write and I want you to be happy."

I longed to ask more questions, but Mama was so peaceful that night I rolled back around and stared at the stars in silence while Mama sang softly in French. I painted in my mind the sweetest dream of a lifetime spent gardening the stars.

Mama had a beautiful voice. It was high and clear. When she sang it sounded like dozens of little tinkling bells. I used to lie awake in bed and listen to her play the piano and sing from the foyer until my eyelids slid down and shut.

For the last six years, it had been the two of us, just like this. I was born when Mama thought she was already an old woman: 1925, the year she turned forty-seven. She always called me her "miracle baby" as a result.

All Mama and I had were each other. Mama said that the world was full of people — and people are full of evil. She told me there was no one and nothing you could trust but where you come from and who you are. We didn't talk to those evil people. We kept to ourselves and spent our time keeping busy.

I heard a meow from across the yard. "Daphne," I whispered, holding out my hands for my little orange kitten. I held her close and whispered in her little feline ears the names of the different constellations. "And that one right there is Taurus — it holds the star Alcyone, just like my name. See, Daphne?" I yawned, smiling. Daphne purred and settled her head on my stomach. I stared at my namesake. "I'm a star, aren't I?"

The moon began to grow hazy and dim as my eyelids started to drop. Mama rubbed my back with one hand and sang to herself as I drifted off to sleep.

* * * * *

Saturday was window-washing day. I was in charge of the downstairs windows, and Mama took care of the upstairs.

I wrung my cloth in the water and created swirly marks on the windowpane. I sighed and let the rag slide down the glass, leaving behind a soapy trail.

Upstairs, I could hear Mama belting out the words to her favorite opera. I rocked back and forth on my heels as I scrubbed the kitchen windows, swishing the rag along with the song.

The doorbell rang.

I dropped my washcloth and ran to the door, pausing to fix my apron and hair. "Who is it?" I called.

"Sam Carroll," came the muffled response.

My shoulders dropped. *Great.* I opened the door and frowned. "What do you want, Sam?"

Sam grinned, handing me a bouquet of wildflowers and a little wrapped parcel. "Happy birthday, Allie."

I sighed. "My birthday isn't until tomorrow."

Sam continued to grin, oblivious to my irritation. "I know. But we're going out of town to visit my aunt Rachel, who lives right on the seashore where you can actually go out and swim and everything, and we won't be back for three weeks, so I thought I'd give you your gift today." He took a deep breath before handing me the parcel, grinning all the while.

I tried to smile back. Now, don't get me wrong. Sam Carroll wasn't a creep or bully or anything. It's just that he was … well, he was *Sam Carroll*, for goodness' sake. I'd only known him for forever and he'd only followed me around for even longer. For nearly fourteen years I'd endured Sam's freckled face and wayward brown hair and adoring blue eyes.

I was kind of sick of him.

"Thanks, Sam," I said, trying to shut the door.

"Alcyone!" Mama called from upstairs.

I grimaced. "Yes, ma'am?"

"Who's at the door?"

"It's just Sam Carroll, Mama!"

"Oh." There was a pause and then Mama was at the door behind me, smiling at Sam. "How lovely of you to drop by, Sam."

"Thank you, Mrs. Everly." Sam pulled his hands out of his pockets and blushed. "I was just dropping off Allie's birthday gift."

"How lovely." Mama stroked my hair and smiled at me. "Alcyone, dear, did you thank Sam?"

Why does she insist on calling me Alcyone whenever company's around? She never does it any other time. I forced another smile. "Thank you, Sam."

"Won't you stay for tea?" Mama asked, wiping her dirty hands on her apron. "We were just about to take a break and enjoy some cookies in the garden."

"Thank you," Sam said, following us into the house.

I glared at Mama's back as we walked through the hall.

"So, Allie, are you turning fourteen?"

Sam. I glanced at him out of the side of my eye, annoyed because he was interrupting my glaring. "Yes."

"Are you having a party?"

I frowned at him. *With what friends?* "No."

"Oh."

Mama led us out into the garden, where a little table was set up with three chairs. *What?*

As if reading my mind, Sam asked, "Who else were you expecting?"

"You," Mama said simply, turning back into the house to get the pitcher of lemonade.

Now that we were alone, Sam pulled out my chair and then sat down next to me. Daphne pranced up and rubbed her head against Sam's leg, and he leaned down to stroke Daphne's furry little head. I turned my glare to her. *Traitor.*

Daphne purred and playfully swatted Sam's hand. Sam laughed. "Hey, watch it!" He sat back and looked around in wonder. "Your garden looks amazing."

It was amazing, of course. *That's what generally happens when you have an unsociable, fantasy-prone mother.*

"Thank you," Mama said, shutting the screen door with a bang. "The roses bloomed nicely this year, didn't they? Alcyone tended them. I didn't touch a single bud, I swear." She smiled at me as she served us lemonade, and I noticed she'd gotten out her best pitcher. I stared at her hands. They were white and smooth, seemingly untouched. I propped my chin up. *How does she keep her hands so pretty?*

Suddenly one of them began to shake. Mama put down the pitcher with a thud and crossed her hands behind her back. She was shivering, though, and she turned her head.

Sam nodded, picking up a giant cookie. "The roses are beautiful."

I glanced across the garden and studied my work. I'd decided long ago to plant nothing but pink and white roses, winding down the garden path and up the old white trellis that shadowed the little gazebo where Mama was married.

Beside the gazebo was a little pond of goldfish surrounded by lilies and guarded by a weathered stone angel. On the other side of the garden were four thin stone pathways, lined with colorful flowers, all leading up to a cushioned little bench.

"Your garden makes my little bouquet seem puny, Mrs. Everly," Sam said, popping a blueberry into his mouth.

"Well, it took years of hard labor to get it this way." Mama beamed and looked over her garden.

And an extremely devoted daughter. I took a bite out of my cookie, washing it down with a sip of lemonade.

"I wanted to create a place where the fairies could play," Mama said softly, still gazing over the flowers, now with a distant look on her face. "Where nothing could go wrong." She twisted her empty ring finger.

I exchanged a glance with Sam, a little embarrassed.

"Mama, would you please pass the cream cheese?" I interrupted.

Mama snapped out of her daze. "Of course, darling."

"These are wonderful cookies," Sam said through a mouthful of food. He gulped and smiled.

"Thank you. It was my grandmother's recipe. She used it during the Civil War."

"Oh?" Sam dabbed his mouth with a napkin.

Uh-oh. Here we go with the Battle of Atlanta. I sunk in my seat. The one thing she had to be able to remember perfectly.

"It was the Battle of Atlanta. In 1864," Mama began, gazing at the sky. "The summer had been unbearably hot. My grandmother thought it would never end."

I grabbed another cookie and ran through different musings in my head, tuning Mama out. I suppose I should have bailed out Sam and changed the subject, but at the moment I didn't feel in any rush to assist him at all. He's the one who got her started on that long story anyway.

I twisted the ring on my pinky finger and thought of words to describe Sam. *Annoying ... nosy ... bothersome ... dopey ...*

"And then he ..." Mama paused, a confused look on her face. Her brow tightened as she concentrated. "He ..."

Sam frowned. "He did what, Mrs. Everly?"

Mama squinted up at the sky. "I can't ... I can't remember."

I glanced at her. "It's okay, Mama. Don't strain yourself." I sat on my hands, resisting the urge to get up and wrap my arms around her.

She frowned, her eyes not meeting mine. "I'm fine."

"Wow," Sam said after a somewhat awkward silence. "What a story."

Mama nodded. "Yes. Grandmother was quite the woman."

Sam nodded, his eyes enthusiastic. "I love war stories. I'm going to be in the army one day too."

"Oh." Mama rubbed her finger along the rim of her glass.

"I'm sorry ... I just wish I could remember ..." She frowned and looked around the table. "Allie, where's the salt shaker?"

I lowered my voice. "Mama, it's right in front of you."

"Oh." Mama rubbed her forehead. "I didn't see it."

Sam nodded again and pushed back from the table. "Thank you so much for the tea, Mrs. Everly. And happy birthday, Allie."

I didn't meet his eye. He was such a goody two-shoes. He didn't deserve to be said good-bye to. *Not in a million years would I ever ...*

"Alcyone," Mama whispered through gritted teeth.

"Good-bye" I looked down.

Sam nodded at us both and walked back toward the house.

"Have fun at your aunt's house," Mama called, waving at him.

I sighed and went inside to practice the piano. The windows could wait a little longer.

* * * * *

"What did that boy give you?"

My head jolted up from my mashed potatoes. "What boy?"

Mama's face glowed from the candlelight that lined the table. We were sitting in the garden, watching the fireflies dance in the cool evening breeze. "Sam."

"Oh." I played with my potatoes. "A sketchbook and chalk set." I made a face. It was exactly what I wanted. Sam *had* been listening when I went on and on about painting on our way home from school last week. *To fill the silence, of course.* I'd already forced down the pleasure from Sam knowing what I wanted and convinced myself he just wanted to annoy me with his obnoxious *niceness*.

"That's nice." Mama pushed her plate away. She sighed to herself and gazed over my shoulder, a strange look on her face.

I continued to mess with my potatoes in silence a few more minutes. "I haven't drawn anything yet," I said finally. "But I'd like to know if you'll pose for me tonight."

"Of course," Mama said. She frowned at something behind me.

I looked over my shoulder, curious as to what she was staring at. There was nothing there except a few blackbirds perched on top of the house.

"Any ideas as to how you'd like me to draw you?"

Mama continued to stare into the distance.

"Mama? Mama!"

Mama's head jerked as she looked around, disoriented. "What—Where am I?"

I reached my arm across the table and stroked her hand. "You're in the garden, Mama. Don't you see?" I massaged her wrist, fighting back worry.

"Hmm?" Mama looked around groggily.

"Mama," I whispered, pulling her up to her feet, "maybe you should go inside for the night."

Mama trudged to the kitchen, muttering to herself, as I cleaned up the dishes in the garden.

When the last of the silverware was put away and the candles were snuffed, I grabbed my notebook and headed out to the hills to watch the sun set.

The countryside of Tennessee was a place of great beauty, one that never ceased to fill my mind. When I sat upon the highest hill, I could see for miles around me, the rolling grass engulfing me in large green pools. The Carroll's little farmhouse, Mr. Ward's old tractors, the Peterson's horses … and my own little house, a quaint smudge in the distance.

I opened up my notebook and took out the new set of chalks Sam gave me. *He'll never have to know I actually used them.*

I flipped to a new page and began to fill in the colors of the sun sinking behind the old white church. Fiery red, burnt orange, creamy yellow.

The only sounds I could hear were the scraping of my chalk over the distant neighing of the horses being led back into their stables.

I bent my head over my drawing and shaded in the vibrant reflection from the pond near the church. My eyes flickered up. The sky was beginning to turn gray.

I held back my notebook to observe the drawing. *Not bad.*

I turned the page and smoothed out the creamy white paper. In the top corner, I wrote,

May 28, 1939.

I wonder if the great poets and artists of the world ever came to Tennessee. I bet that if they had, the beauty of these hills and farms would have been drawn all over their minds for years to come. I know that they will always be drawn on mine.

Sometimes, when I come up here, I feel like I'm closer to God. Or the heavens. I've never told Mama that. She doesn't think that God exists—doesn't believe in a life after death. I know I should believe her, that I shouldn't question anything she says, but yet I still wonder. What is there outside this tiny world and all our short lifetimes?

I wish I had a friend.

I flipped the notebook shut and laid back on the grass, listening to my heart beat until everything around me was nearly dark. Then I stumbled back home and tucked myself into bed.

Chapter 2

New feet within my garden go,
New fingers stir the sod;
A troubadour upon the elm
Betrays the solitude.

—Emily Dickinson

$\mathcal{I}$t was a scream that woke me. I jolted up in bed, my senses pulsing. *What was that?*

There it was again—a bloodcurdling shriek. "Get away from me!"

Mama! I jumped out of bed and threw open the door, running down the hall. I burst into Mama's doorway and stood, chest heaving.

Mama was standing on her bed, her eyes wide with fright. "Get it!" she cried. "Oh, Allie, take it away!"

I looked around the room and blinked. Nothing. "Get what?" I finally asked.

"The bird!" Mama shrieked, hurling her pillow at the vanity. "The snake! Oh, Allie, it must have gotten in through the window!"

I looked at the window. It was closed.

With an eye on Mama, I inched toward the vanity. Mama's hair stood up like a madwoman, her face as pale as her nightgown.

I picked up the pillow she had thrown and scooped up the broken shards of glass. "Oh no," I muttered. A perfume bottle had broken. Liquid ran down the dresser, staining the pure white wood.

"Is it gone?"

"Yes, Mama." I threw the glass shards into the wastebasket. My breath caught and I glanced down to see blood trickling down my finger. I pressed it in my pajamas and bit my lip. "It went away. Back out the window."

"Is it coming back?"

I turned and looked at my mother. The terror and anger had left from her face, and now she stood on the bed, shaking. Her tangled hair fell across her face as she dropped the pillow she'd been clinging to. Then, without a word, she collapsed on her knees and broke into tears.

I rushed across the room and put my arm around her, rocking her back and forth. "It's okay, Mama," I whispered into her hair. "It's okay."

"Its eyes were so cold, Allie," Mama sobbed into my lap. "They were staring right at me."

"I know." I stared at the empty vanity, illuminated by moonlight. "It's gone now."

"Allie?" Mama whimpered.

"Yes?"

She looked up at me with bloodshot eyes and gripped my hand. "Will you stay with me tonight?"

I gulped down the lump in my throat and nodded. "Of course, Mama. I'll stay."

I stroked Mama's hair and sang to her softly until she fell asleep. Tears stung behind my eyes, threatening to overflow.

I buried my face in the pillow. No one else knew. No one else would ever know. I was all Mama needed.

In the morning, she'd forget all about the snake. She always did. Maybe she'd have a good day again and she'd be able to laugh and chat.

Or maybe she'd have a bad day.

No, I couldn't think about that. There would be no more bad days. As long as I stayed with her, Mama would get better.

Help her remember, the doctor said. Read her favorite books. Sing her favorite songs.

I'd done it. I'd read the books. I'd sung the songs. And she still wasn't better.

I clenched my fists and stuck one in my mouth to stop the tears.

"Allie?" Mama whispered.

"Yes, ma'am?" I wiped my nose on my sleeve.

"I'm thirsty."

I kicked my feet out of bed and went downstairs to get her some milk from the icebox. By the time I got back, she was asleep again.

I crawled into bed beside her and cried until my eyes couldn't stay open anymore.

* * * *

"Happy birthday to you! Happy birthday to you! Happy birthday, dear Allie! Happy birthday to you!"

Mama clapped while I blew out the fourteen candles on my little white cake. The living room was decorated with a few balloons I'd blown up and some old pieces of fabric tied to the staircase like streamers. Mama scooped me into a hug and left the dining room, muttering about a cake carver.

I was left alone, staring at the smoking candles. Fourteen years, come and gone. My mouth twitched in a deflated smile.

"Here it is!" Mama announced, coming back into the kitchen with a knife. She flourished it with pleasure and reached out a hand. "My lady, if you please."

I placed a plate in her hand and watched as she carved out two thick pieces of red velvet cake. I took a big bite and closed my eyes. *Heaven.*

"To eleven years of Alcyone!" Mama smiled, holding up her plate.

"Fourteen years." I stared at my fork. "I'm fourteen years old today."

"Oh, right." Mama blinked. She sighed and rubbed the bags under her eyes.

"I was thinking," I said, swallowing my bite of cake. "Maybe I'll play the piano for you this evening. You could rest on the couch and I could play whatever you'd like."

"That'd be nice." Mama's voice had that distracted sound again.

I tried to catch her eye, determined not to lose her attention. "I drew a picture with my new chalks last night. Would you like to see it?"

Mama didn't answer. She'd tuned out into one of her moods.

I took another bite of red velvet cake and stared at the wallpaper. It was purple with white flowers, which I'd always thought was a bit odd. But it was Mama's house to decorate, not mine.

After we ate, I led Mama into the drawing room and let her lay down on the sofa. We read for a while, and then she asked me to play the piano.

The keys felt cold and slippery beneath my fingers. When I was little, I'd sit in that same spot for hours, practicing and practicing while Mama sat on the couch, her eyes rarely straying from my hands. Now she snored lightly, oblivious to the noise.

Within half an hour, Mama had dozed off, a wet washcloth on her forehead from the headache she complained of earlier. She had dressed herself that morning—pulling a dirty dress on over her nightgown and fastening the bursting buttons with six different brooches.

I kept playing for hours after Mama had fallen asleep. I don't know why I did, but it just felt right. To keep on playing, no matter what.

I played Chopin first. Then Mozart. Then Liszt.

After awhile, the muscles in my hands began to ache. I shut the piano and looked down at the closed cover. I hadn't noticed how dark the room had gotten.

＊ ＊ ＊ ＊ ＊

"I'm back, Allie."

I knew the voice even before I saw who it belonged to. "Hello, Sam." I didn't look up from the roses.

"I don't know if you remember, but I told you I was going to my aunt Rachel's house three weeks ago."

"I remember." I stood up, shook out my gloves, and flopped on my sunhat. I squinted at Sam in the afternoon sun.

His freckled face was scrubbed and his skinny little arms were stuck in his pockets. "Can I help?"

I turned and knelt by the pansies, not the slightest bit ruffled to be caught in the old, muddy overalls I was wearing. I wiped my cheek with the back of my glove. "It's a free country."

Sam stooped down beside me, getting dirt on his fresh blue jeans. He weeded the pansies for what felt like half an hour, without a word. It was like some kind of miracle.

I kept stealing glances over my shoulder to see if Mama had awoken from her spot on the back porch. She hadn't.

"How was your birthday?" Sam asked.

I jumped a little, startled at his voice. Then I blushed and looked down so that my straw hat would cover my face. "Good."

"Whadja get?"

Well, I got some chalk from you. I pulled another weed. "Nothing. We just made some cake and sang."

Sam wrinkled his nose. "You mean your mama doesn't get you any presents for your birthday?"

I pulled the weeds harder. "She is my present." *At least, every day I have left with her is.*

"Oh." Sam seemed to frown to himself. "Yeah, I didn't get much for mine either. Daddy said that ever since the government took all our money, we're not gonna have much to spend for a while. I guess it's that way for everyone else too."

I nodded, only half listening. I patted the dirt around the pansies back into place, then sat back to admire my work.

Purple and yellow and burgundy splashes of color filled the little flower bed.

"Ouch," Sam said under his breath.

I looked up to catch him grimacing at his hand. But when he saw me watching him, he quickly hid it behind his back.

"Let me see," I ordered, holding out my hand.

He paused a moment before pulling his arm out and showing me his palm. I gasped. It was covered with red welts and cuts. *From pulling my weeds.*

I cleared my throat and dropped his hand. "You'd better come in and get some medicine for that."

Sam followed me into the house. "Up on the counter," I commanded. Sam climbed up and perched on the cold countertop, watching me silently.

I rinsed his wounds with cool water and rubbed some of Mama's salve on them. Then I bent beneath the sink and pulled out some clean rags, ripping one into shreds so I could wrap it around Sam's hand.

"You're not like most people, are you?" Sam's voice sounded curious.

"I don't know. I haven't met most people." I bit my lower lip. "There," I said, patting the poorly bandaged hand. "All done." I looked over my work, feeling like a saint.

I looked up to see Sam staring at me.

"What?" I asked.

"You're awful pretty, Allie," Sam whispered.

I gave him a little smile, feeling too charitable at the moment to be annoyed. "Good-bye, Sam," I said instead. "And thank you for the help with the pansies. They don't look as bad as I thought they would … you know, with you helping and all." I cleared my throat.

Sam jumped off the counter and shook my hand with his good one before walking out the door. "Good-bye, Allie."

I rolled my eyes before going back out to the garden.

* * * * *

I opened my notebook and smoothed down the fresh page. Even without looking up, I could tell Mama was watching me from her seat in the armchair.

June 18, 1939

Well, today was a wonderful day. Mama and I worked in the garden and made pancakes and cleaned the kitchen floors together. Mama is so happy; it makes me feel all warm and tingly inside.

"What are you writing?"

I looked up, surprised by the coldness of Mama's tone. She was glowering at me, the light extinguished in her blue eyes.

"Nothing, Mama." I lifted the journal so she could see. "I'm just writing in my diary."

Mama wrapped her favorite blanket around her tightly and pursed her lips. "What are you writing about?" Her voice began to grow tense. "Are you writing about me, Allie? What are you saying about me?"

"Mama, calm down." I reached out a hand toward her. Her eyes widened as she flinched away. My hand suddenly felt cold and empty, suspended in the air. I clenched my fist and let it drop.

26

I read aloud what I had written. But by the time I lifted my head, Mama was staring at the clock on the wall, her face expressionless.

"Allie?" she asked after a few moments.

"Yes?"

"Can we go on a picnic tomorrow? Invite that boy, Sam. Tell him to go on a picnic with us tomorrow."

"Yes, Mama." I looked down.

Mama stared at me. "Call him now. He might forget."

I sighed and reached for the telephone on the table. *This is going to be embarrassing.*

Sam answered. "Hello?"

I fidgeted with my skirt. "Um, hello. This is Allie Everly."

There was a pause. And then, "Oh, hi, Allie!"

My face reddened. Thank heavens he couldn't see *that* over the telephone. "Mama wanted me to call and invite you on a picnic tomorrow. By the pond, I guess. She's packing a lunch and everything."

"That sounds like fun." Sam's voice grew excited. "What time are you having it?"

I glanced at Mama, who had fallen back asleep. "Probably at noon."

"Great!" There was an awkward silence. "Okay. See you tomorrow, Allie."

The line clicked dead. I sighed and placed the telephone back on the retriever. Mama snored lightly from the sofa. *She looks . . .*

I gulped down the liquid in my throat and glanced back down at the journal page. A tear escaped my eye and smeared a fresh stroke of ink. I groaned and blew on the page.

Oh, I'm just so happy! We're both just so happy in the summer!

I closed the notebook with a slam and left to do the dishes.

* * * * *

The water felt deliciously cold, licking my bare toes. I smiled and let my foot make little swirls across the surface of the lake.

I paused and tapped my pen to my mouth. *What's a descriptive word for love?* I racked my brain. *Adoration ... affection ... fondness ... devotion ...*

I smiled and began scribbling in my notebook again. *Devotion.*

My hand began to cramp. That was always a sign that it was time to stop for the day.

I massaged my fingers and read over the poem. "Mama."

It was the perfect description of her. I smiled and lifted my toes out of the water, hugging them to my chest. *She'd love to hear it.*

"Allie!" Mama called. "Sam's here!"

Raising myself off the little wooden dock, I scooped up my journal and shoes. Beside me, Daphne purred and stretched out. I laughed and nudged her with my foot. "Come on, lazy-head."

I walked back through the apple grove, struggling to carry my things. Bending under a twisted branch, I smiled at the two-some sitting on a little blanket.

"Hello." Sam's grin seemed to stretch forever. His dark hair was mussed and there were dirt stains on his trousers. I wondered if he'd been working outside.

"I packed a lunch," Mama said, motioning to a basket. It

was her tradition. She always packed the lunch, and I never interfered. Never.

I picked up a jar. "Is that why you brought homemade relish?"

Mama nodded and smoothed out her dress. Her blue eyes looked so hopeful and expectant.

I sighed and sat on the blanket. "Very well. We'll eat what Mama packed." I opened the basket and looked inside. *Mayonnaise ... jelly ... pickled onions ... canned peaches ...*

"Mama, did you bring any bread?"

Mama shook her head, blinking.

I cursed myself. *I should have known she couldn't pack lunch by herself. She can't do anything by herself.* I forced a smile. "Oh, well." I pulled out the jar of peaches. "We'll feast on peaches and pickled onions. That is, if you don't mind, Sam."

Sam shook his head. "I love canned peaches."

I screwed open the lid and pulled out a slippery peach. Mama reached out and devoured it in a single gulp. I frowned. "Be careful not to choke."

I pulled out a peach for myself. Sticky sweetness slid down my throat. I licked my lips. "Yummy. We sure did a good job on these."

Mama smiled softly. "Yes, we did. David always says I don't cut the peaches small enough, but he doesn't know anything." Her brow creased. "Allie, did I cut the peaches small enough?"

You didn't cut them at all. I did. I cleared my throat and glanced at Sam. He was studying Mama, his brow furrowing. "Yes, you cut them small enough," I answered.

Mama nodded and placed her hands in her lap. "David was going to join us, but I couldn't find him in the study." She frowned at me. "When I can't find him, it's always because he's in the study."

What in the world is she talking about? I put down the jar of peaches and gently touched Mama's wrist. "Daddy isn't here anymore, remember?" My voice lowered. "He left six years ago."

"Oh." Mama smiled. "Well, I don't care, because I know I cut the peaches small enough!"

I patted her wrist. "Yes, and they're very good."

Sam nodded. "Best peaches I've ever had!" He wiped juice off his cheek and shone that ridiculous grin at me.

I reached into the picnic basket for the jar of pickled onions. "Onion?"

Mama didn't answer.

I looked up to find her staring in stony silence at the water. "Mama? What's wrong?"

She glanced at me. "I refuse to eat with a stranger staring at me."

"What are you— " I sighed. "No one's staring at you."

Mama raised a dark eyebrow and glanced at a duck sitting on the glassy pond. I rolled my eyes. "A duck?"

"It's watching us, Allie." Mama folded her hands. "It's waiting." She shivered. "I won't eat while it's staring at me."

I sighed and put down the jar of onions, climbing to my feet. My heartbeat fluttered as I glanced at Sam. He clambered up and brushed off his pants. "I'll help you wrangle the duck."

I glared at him. "Thank you ever so much."

With one last glance at Mama, I grabbed my shoes and trudged across the orchard.

The duck stared at us in silence as it glided across the surface of the lake. "Go. Shoo." I waved at it. *This is ridiculous.*

Sam snorted. "Shoo! Shoo! Shoo!" He began waving his arms above his head and jumping about. "Shoo!"

The duck continued to stare at us, unfazed.

I looked back at Mama. She watched me, her hands in her lap. The duck obviously had to go.

I dropped my shoes on the dock. *Here goes.* I lifted a foot and cautiously placed it in the water, squeezing my eyes shut. *How am I going to get the duck if I can't swim?*

I peeked an eye open and lowered my voice. "Please go before she throws a fit." *Great. Now I'm talking to a duck.* I bit my lip. "It's for your own good, I promise you."

The duck stared at me and swam around in smooth circles. *Is it mocking me?*

My face began to grow hot. I reached an arm out and pushed at the bird, attempting to physically shove it away.

The duck jumped up and flapped its wings in a fury, honking loudly as it advanced in our direction. I screamed and in my panic hurled myself backward, landing in the water. I yelled again as the ice-cold water seeped through my thin dress.

Sam was hollering, half from fear and half from laughter. "Run, Allie! Run!"

I scrambled to my feet and took off behind Sam. The duck followed, his feathers ruffling.

The apple orchard had never seemed so immense. I ran through the trees, looking over my shoulder. The duck had finally stopped and was strutting around the pond, the obvious victor.

I collapsed on the picnic blanket and wrung out my soaking skirt. *Darned fowl.*

"Mama, the duck can't go. I … uh …" I licked my lips. "I spoke to it and it …"

Mama blinked, smiling at me.

My shoulders slumped. "Never mind." *I guess I won't have to worry about duck-filled dreams tonight.*

Sam was snorting in laughter, grabbing his stomach. "That was … that was priceless! The look on your face! You were talking to a duck!" He rolled onto his back. "Oh, this is so nice." He sighed, a satisfied look spreading across his face.

"Glad you think so," I muttered. I sat back and looked around the orchard. The ripening apples swung from the trees, wobbling in the wind.

"Allie, are those your shoes?"

I followed Mama's glance and saw my shoes still sitting on the dock. I sighed. "Yes." Focusing on Mama, I stood and took a step back. "Stay right here on the blanket. I'll only be a minute."

I ran down the hill to the lake and scooped my shoes off the dock. The duck was still gliding across the water, staring at me blankly. I rolled my eyes. "Stupid duck." I stood back and watched it take off in flight.

Sighing, I turned and trudged back up toward the picnic blanket. I squinted at the sun. It was getting late. I paused. The picnic blanket was empty. Mama wasn't there.

"Allie!" Sam shouted.

I dropped my shoes. My heart began to race. I whipped around and scanned the orchard. "Where are you?"

Someone sneezed. I ran in the direction of the sound, my shoulders dropping once I approached the source. *Mama.*

She was perched in a tree, reaching for an unripe apple. She looked down and brightened. "Oh, Allie. Can you help me reach this apple?"

I ran up beside Sam and stood at the base of the tree, grabbing one of Mama's dangling legs. "Come down from there," I said calmly, although my pulse was throbbing. "Climbing trees isn't safe, remember?"

Mama licked her lips, looking panicked. "I ... I can't."

"What do you mean?" I forced my voice to sound light and teasing. "You got up there, didn't you?"

She began to mumble to herself about being dizzy. She swayed, reaching out to grab the trunk for support. "Allie ... my head. It feels ..." Her voice was slurred.

I took a shaky breath and began to climb the tree. The wood was too smooth, too slick. *How did she get up there in the first place?*

"Grab my hand," I said, extending an arm to her. "I'll get you down."

Mama stared at me with her large blue eyes. "What?"

"Give me your hand."

She recoiled as if I were a poisonous adder, slamming her head against the trunk of the tree. "Get your hand away from me!"

I winced at the impact of her skull against the wood. But Mama wasn't crying, wasn't even moaning. The only emotion on her face was fear of me. She was terrified of her daughter.

"Mama ..." My voice cracked. I licked my lips. "Please. Give me your hand. We're going home now."

Mama began to cry, the tears streaking her pale cheeks. "Get away from me!" She buried her face in her sleeve. "I won't go anywhere with you!"

She's going to fall. She's going to get hurt. I glanced down and began to panic. We weren't very high, but the ground was just far enough away to cause damage if she lost her balance. "Stop this nonsense!" I tried to grab her wrist. "Come on. At least let me pull you down."

She turned her head from me and sobbed into her arm. "Go away!"

My heart sank. *She really doesn't know who I am.*

"Okay," I whispered, releasing her wrist. I climbed down the tree and settled in the grass. Peering up at Mama, I let out a long sigh. "If you're not going to come down, I'm just going to wait."

"I'll never come down!" Mama sniffled. "I . . . I . . ." She gasped for breath. "I told you I cut the peaches small enough! I did, I did." She covered her face with her hands, muffling her sobs.

I lowered my eyes and sank onto the ground, picking up a stick to trace patterns in the dirt.

Sam squatted beside me, leaning against the tree. "Allie, I . . ."

Mama choked on a sob, then began to quiet down. Her shoulders were still shaking, but her breathing slowed.

I glanced at Sam. He was watching me, his blue eyes brimming with tears. I looked away.

"Allie?" Sam whispered.

"What?" I jabbed at the ground with the stick. *Stupid dirt.*

"I'm sorry."

Those two words hung in the air — punctuated by Mama's stifled cries. "So am I," I whispered, curling my knees up to my chest.

"Can I . . ." Sam bit his lip, then reached out to touch my hair. "Is there anything I can do?"

I jerked away. "No."

"Oh." His face fell. He dropped his hand and stuck it in his pocket. "I guess I'll go."

"Okay."

He stood and lingered for only a second before turning away. I looked up at his back and bit my lip. "Sam?"

He turned. "Yeah?"

"Thanks for coming to the picnic." I gave him a small smile.

He grinned slowly, his blue eyes crinkling. "I had a good time."

I watched him walk away before I picked up my stick again, drawing letters in the dirt.

* * * * *

I looked up at the rose-painted sky. Shots of amber and gold lit up the pond, casting shadows through the speckled leaves of the apple trees.

A soft snore came from the tree. I looked up and saw Mama's leg swaying back and forth—dangling from the branch.

Releasing a heavy breath, I pushed myself up, brushing dirt off my skirt. I bit my lip, staring at Mama. *How am I going to get her down?*

I managed to clamber halfway up the tree and wrap my arms around her waist. Careful to keep her head from hitting any branches, I pulled her sleeping body out of the tree and laid it on the picnic blanket.

There was a nasty bump on the back of her head, so I ran back to the house and scooped ice cubes out of the icebox, wrapping them in an old rag. Kneeling by Mama's side, I pressed the rag against her skull.

Oh, Mama, why? Why are you doing this to yourself?

Tears stung at my eyes. I whispered, "At least you fell asleep in our own backyard. I can't imagine how I would have gotten you home from Mr. Ward's house." I smoothed a dark hair off her forehead.

"I love you," I whispered. I cleared my throat. "Do you remember … do you remember when I was little and I used to draw you pictures, and they were absolutely awful but you used to tell me they were beautiful and hang them above the dining room table? Then we'd pretend we had guests over and you'd make them praise me too."

A lump formed in my throat. I looked down at Mama and smiled, stroking her soft cheek. "They should have praised you instead."

I pulled off my sweater and wrapped it around Mama's thin shoulders. Then I curled up on the ground next to her, holding her hand against my cheek.

✳ ✳ ✳ ✳ ✳

The June sky was so blue. I leaned against the sturdy tree trunk and stared up at it, fingering my apple. A flock of birds appeared on the horizon and called out to each other as they crossed over the yard. I wondered what it would be like to be a bird, wild and free. *What a delicious afternoon.* A smile spread across my face, warm and slow.

"When are we going to decorate for Christmas, Allie?"

I frowned and looked down, jerked back to reality. Mama was sitting below me on a blanket, a book in her lap. This one was full of pictures, since her eyes couldn't focus on the words anymore.

"Mama, it's still summer."

Mama shook her head. "No it's not, it's Christmastime." She squinted up at me.

I took another bite of my apple and rested my head up against the oak tree. My bare legs swung through the humid summer air. "Mama, if it were almost Christmas, wouldn't we be wearing coats?"

Mama frowned for a minute, her clear blue eyes looking very troubled. "No."

"Okay, then." I munched my apple and looked up at the sky. Dark clouds were beginning to gather, threatening a storm. Perhaps I had better get Mama inside.

"We need to get out our Christmas album, Allie."

I looked down. Mama was staring up at me with that stern look on her face.

I tried to decide which would be worse: having the neighbors think we were crazy or disappointing Mama. "Okay," I sighed, swinging down from the tree.

I put in one of Mama's old record albums and waltzed around the living room with her to "Silent Night."

"Allie," Mama moaned, "you're stepping on my toes."

"Sorry." I played the male part, leading Mama around the room. *One-two-three, one-two-three.* Mama's waist felt so thin and frail; I had to dig my fingers into her sides to hold on. *Where did all her flesh go?*

"Ouch." This time Mama stepped on my foot.

My head was getting dizzy as we spun around the room. Mama was staring at the walls behind me, paying no attention to her feet or her partner. I frowned, beginning to feel sulky.

"Do you think we're finished now?" I asked as "Silent Night" turned into "Winter Wonderland." I put my hand on my forehead and pushed back my bangs. Mama looked uncertain.

"Did we hear 'Away in a Manger'?"

Three sharp knocks rapped on the door.

Mama's face lit up as she moved toward the hall. "Oh, is that—?"

I dashed in front of her and smiled. "That's for me," I said, leading her back to the couch. "Stay right here until I get back."

I opened the door to find our neighbor, Mrs. Peterson, peering over my shoulder, her glasses sliding down her nose. "Why, hello, Allie." She glanced toward the living room, her interest clearly piqued. "Is that Christmas music?"

I moved to block her view and plastered on my happiest face. "We like to get in the spirit early."

Mrs. Peterson frowned, then she shrugged her shoulders. "I see," she simpered. "Well, anyway, I just wanted to give you this present, Allie." She handed me a finely wrapped parcel and looked pleased, reaching up to touch the top of her fancy department store hat.

My birthday was three weeks ago, Miss Prissy-Pants. At least Sam got the month right. "Thank you." I hugged the present to my chest and stared at her.

"Well, aren't you going to invite me in?" Mrs. Peterson made a move toward the door.

I quickly stepped in front of her and softened my eyes. "Mama's not feeling very well today," I whispered, tipping my head forward. "Come back tomorrow." I straightened and offered a grin. "But thank you for the gift."

Mrs. Peterson's shocked expression stayed frozen as I shut the door in her face. I locked it and made a face at the wood, feeling better already.

"Who was that?" Mama called from the living room.

"Mrs. Peterson. She just wanted to give me this birthday gift. It's three weeks late, though." I raised my eyes to the ceiling and put the gift on the mantle.

Mama shook her head. "No, it's a Christmas gift." She reached up to rub her neck, pulling at the collar of her flannel nightgown. She must have been heated up given the actual season.

I sighed. "Mama, it's not Christmastime." *Dr. Murphy didn't tell me whether or not I could talk sense into her.*

"Yes, it is. Now open it."

With her calm blue eyes fixed on me, I opened up Mrs. Peterson's well-wrapped gift and grimaced. "Oh, great. A stuffed bear." *To go with the other six identical bears I have from every birthday of mine Mrs. Peterson has ever witnessed.*

"How wonderful," Mama said mechanically. "You should name him Bear."

Wonderful.

Mama crossed her arms and snuggled back in an armchair. She sighed. "I wish David was here." She glanced up at me. "When do you think David will get here?"

My stomach ached. I turned around and placed the bear on the fireplace mantle so Mama wouldn't see my face. "He's not coming back, Mama. He left years ago, remember?"

Mama's eyes filled with tears. "But he loves me. He told me he loves me."

I leaned over and squeezed her hand. "Of course he loves you." I rubbed her arm. "Now you sit here while I get us something to eat, okay?"

It was easier to let Mama think good things about my father than hint at the truth. I could still remember the day he left. It wasn't dramatic, or even sad. A little bitter maybe, but at least they never screamed at each other. Though the only person they ever said I love you to was me, never each other—they both claimed they didn't believe in true love. One day, he decided he didn't love either of us, and told us he was going to leave. And that was it. No fireworks, no bullets, no fights. Mama didn't even cry—at least not in front of me. I did, every night for a month. But neither of us ever talked about it. Ever.

Mama tolerated people and even liked some, but she never loved them. My father was a Christian, or at least he said he was, so now we hated Christians. "They're hateful people," Mama told me the day after he left. "They will make you feel loved—make you feel wanted. But they don't mean any of it. Always remember, look out for yourself and don't let your guard down. Don't ever forget your roots or your common sense."

Mama was still sitting at the table, staring at her hands. I bet she didn't remember any of that anymore. I suggested she sit in the living room and listen to more Christmas music while I fixed supper. Green beans and chicken. Again.

At least I know how to make more than just sandwiches this year, I thought as I set the table. Mrs. Peterson's old cookbooks had been useful after all, and it was nice of her to give them to me. *But really, a fourteen-year-old can only do so much.*

I stood back to get a good look at the table. As an afterthought, I searched the cabinet for some candles to place in the center, and a little lace doily to set them on. *Nice.* I smiled, thinking about Christmas dinner.

"Mama!" I called, pulling off my apron and putting it back on the hook. No answer. "Mama, dinner's ..." I paused in the doorway of the living room. Mama was fast asleep on the couch, curled up in a little ball.

She's barely ever awake lately. I sighed and reached for the old green quilt to lay over her. My hand brushed her cheek as I pushed her hair off her face. It was ashy and hollow.

I turned to leave, peeking at her once more. Mama shivered and pulled the blanket closer. My heart tugged at the sight of my mother wrapped up like a defenseless babe.

"Oh well," I whispered to Daphne, scooping her up in my arms. "I suppose it's just you and me."

I sat Daphne on Mama's lap and stared at her in silence as some woman droned "We wish you a Merry Christmas."

Lonely ... sad ... lost ... I turned off the lights in the kitchen and sat down in the dark. Mama's empty plate was in front of me. I took a small bite of my green beans before pushing the food away and clearing the table instead.

Chapter 3

I felt a funeral in my brain,
And mourners, to and fro,
Kept treading, treading, till it seemed
That sense was breaking through.

—Emily Dickinson

A llie?"

I lowered my book. Mama looked up at me with tired eyes. I jumped up from my seat and knelt on the floor beside the couch. "Yes?"

Mama reached out and took my hand in hers—her palms felt cool and clammy. She squeezed my hand and smiled faintly, her eyes crinkling like they used to. "I love you, my little miracle baby." Her voice sounded breathless.

I smiled back. "And I love you too."

Mama took a deep breath and leaned back. "This headache …" She paused and licked her lips, "This headache has really made me tired. I … I wanted to know if you would read me another poem, Allie."

"Of course." I squeezed her palm, glad to hear her speaking my name. "What do you want to hear?"

Mama closed her eyes and sighed. "Dickinson. 'The Heart Asks Pleasure First.'"

I was pleasantly surprised that she remembered the name of her favorite poem. That was progress, right?

"My heart wants to die," Mama said softly.

My head jerked up. "What?"

She shook her head and looked away. I stared at her for a few more seconds in silence. It had never occurred to me that Mama might welcome the thought of death, since she didn't believe in anything beyond that. Wouldn't that cause you to fear the end?

The idea chilled me. I tried to put it out of my head as I crossed my legs and flipped through the volume of poetry in my lap, turning to Mama's favorite.

> "The heart asks pleasure first,
> And then, excuse from pain;
> And then, those little anodynes
> That deaden suffering;
> And then, to go to sleep;
> And then, if it should be
> The will of its Inquisitor,
> The liberty to die."

I shut the book and ran my hand over the worn cover. "Well, that was Emily Dickinson for you."

The candlelight flickered across Mama's sleeping face.

I sighed and laid the book down in my lap.

"I hope you enjoyed it, Mama. Dickinson is your favorite." I fingered the fraying spine of the slim book of poems. I flipped through the dog-eared pages, held it close to smell the fading scent of Mama. "Do you remember reading this to me, Mama?" My voice faded to a whisper as I let my fingers slide off the cover. "Do you remember?"

Mama rolled on her side and mumbled something in her sleep. The moment was over; she was lost again. I kissed her cheek and sat back down.

"Why are you so tired all the time?" I whispered. My chest ached looking at her. "I miss talking with you."

I rocked back and forth and looked out the window. Rain trickled down the glass. I followed the dribble of water with my finger. *Funny how much raindrops look like tears.*

Footsteps pounded on the front porch. I started, my book falling out of my lap. I reached down to pick it up and held it close as I inched my way to the front door, where footsteps had been replaced by loud raps on the door. I glanced out the window. A figure dressed in a dark slicker was standing out front with a large bag in his hand.

There had to be something I could use as a weapon. Why did we have to have such a prissy, safe living room? Finally, I grabbed Mama's big black umbrella.

Holding the umbrella out in front of me, I inched my way toward the door. *Deep breaths, Allie. You can do this. Deep breaths.*

My hand hovered over the doorknob for a brief moment before I flung the door open and screamed, waving around my umbrella.

A boy shouted and fell down the steps.

"Sam?" I dropped the umbrella and rushed from the door. "I'm so sorry. Sam? Are you okay?'

He groaned and held his leg. "Allie!"

"I'm so, so sorry!" I knelt on the muddy ground next to him, the rain pouring down my head. "Oh my goodness, Sam, I didn't mean to …" I trailed off, my cheeks reddening, although I'm sure he couldn't see them in the dark. "I thought you were a criminal."

"Do I look like a criminal?" Sam rolled his eyes. "Didn't your mother tell you I was coming? We telephoned her."

"No, I …" I wrung my hands, flustered. "No, I guess not."

Sam held up a paper bag. "My mom thought I might send you all some eggs." Liquid oozed out of the bottom of the bag, and it wasn't from the rain. "Only now they're broken."

I sat on the ground and groaned. I could feel the rain and mud soaking through my skirt. "I'm so, so sorry."

A smile twitched on Sam's face. "You said that."

"I know, but I still am." I buried my head in my wet hands, feeling mortified.

Sam laughed outright and pulled me up. Well, sort of—since, at fourteen years, I was still taller than him. "Aw, shake it off." He handed me the dripping bag and grinned. "Here are your eggs." He tipped his hat. "Good night."

"Wait."

Sam turned around. My stomach squirmed at the thought of what I was about to do.

"You might as well come in and dry off. At least until the rain stops a little." I straightened my shoulders. "As payment. For the … egg mush." I held up the bag and smiled.

Sam pulled off his muddy boots and followed me inside. I wrung out his jacket and hat while he made his way to the living room.

I tipped over a boot and gawked at the amount of water that poured out. It was really pouring out there. I shook my head and placed the boots on a mat, reaching for his hat.

"Is this Christmas music?" Sam called from the living room.

"Yep." Gosh, the hat had almost as much water as the boots.

"What's your mom—Uh, Allie? Allie! Allie, come here! Your mom's—"

I raced into the living room and screamed.

Mama was strewn on the floor, her head on the hardwood and her legs still sliding off the couch.

"Mama!" I shrieked, trying to run to her. My knees began to feel like putty. I groaned, watching the room spin around me. Without a word, my knees gave and I collapsed on the floor.

*****

You see, Mama was sick. Very sick.

I'd first taken her to Dr. Murphy the summer before, when Mama began to misplace things and forget where she was. She was so mad that for a whole week afterward she wouldn't speak to me. But I never told her what the doctor said once the door was closed and we were alone.

Dr. Murphy told me I was to take care of Mama. For however much time she had left.

He claimed I was too old to be lied to, and that I needed to face things as they were and make her last days as comfortable as possible. Because no matter what I did, she would get worse.

Mama was dying.

Dr. Murphy said that Mama showed all the symptoms of brain cancer. Possibly even a tumor. The specifics of the sickness were fuzzy—it varied from patient to patient, so I needed to be prepared for anything.

I'd wanted to take Mama to a special hospital so she could get better. I'd even crawled under the bed and ripped out the seams of the mattress, grabbing the envelope of money I'd seen Mama hide the summer before. I counted it twice, but it still wasn't enough. Only fifty dollars.

Dr. Murphy told me that without treatment Mama would decline quickly until I would have to feed her and dress her and take care of her. He'd seen it happen dozens of times before. And, at some time or another, they always died.

My job was to make her happy—to keep her with us. He said as long as Mama could remember she'd be fine. But she couldn't remember.

* * * * *

"Allie?" a voice asked gently. "Allie, wake up. Wake up, Allie."

Lights all around me. Blurry. Dancing.

I moaned and put my hand on my brow. A giant knot was formed on my forehead. So that's what was causing the pain.

I opened my eyes a little wider and then squinted. *Where in the world*—

"Allie? Oh, she's awake!"

Dr. Murphy was standing above me, the familiar, doctorish smell of aftershave and metal lingering in the air. Dr. Murphy's gray eyes twinkled as he gave my hand a little squeeze. "That a girl. Wake on up, Allie."

I tried to sit up, but the pressure in my head pulled me back down to the pillow.

"Whoa, whoa." Dr. Murphy tightened his grip on my hand. "Steady. Steady."

I looked around. I was in the hospital, in one of those little patient beds. All around me were nurses scribbling on pads of paper. There were other patients in the beds around me, moaning or vomiting, watching me.

I glanced at the doctor and grabbed his coat. "Why am I here? What happened?"

"Ah," Dr. Murphy looked around and nodded his white head. "Momentary confusion and memory loss. It's quite common with mild concussions."

One of the nurses nodded and scribbled something on her notepad.

Dr. Murphy turned back to me and squeezed my hand. "You fell down," he said in a loud voice. "On the floor. Remember?"

What is all this about? I tried to sit up again, a sudden thought piercing through my head. "Where's Mama?"

Dr. Murphy touched my wrist. "She's all right. For now." He glanced at his notepad, which he quickly whipped out of my sight. "She had a bump on the head." He glanced up at me, his eyes probing. "Alcyone ... do you know of anything your mother could have been doing that may have caused her to fall off the couch? We talked about this sickness. Is there anything — any medicines, any treatments that you've been giving her that we haven't prescribed?"

I shook my head, my hands clammy. "No, sir."

Dr. Murphy sighed and pulled off his spectacles. He reached into his coat pocket and pulled out a bottle of pills. "Alcyone, we think your mother may have been suffering a lack of memory and took some pills we prescribed for her to use years ago. That may have accounted for her unconsciousness and fall." His voice grew soft. "Her health is deteriorating. Surely you must know that."

I looked around the doctor's office. The nurses frowned, their eyes sad. I clamped my hands together and took a deep breath. I didn't need their sympathy. They could keep it and waste it on all the puppies and babies in the world, for all I cared. Mama was strong and so was I. She would survive a hundred more Christmases.

"What do you need me to do, doctor?" My voice shook a little. *Coward.* I hated myself for feeling so afraid.

Dr. Murphy sighed and avoided my eyes. "There's nothing else you can do. It's just a matter of time." He took a deep breath. "I'd like ... I'd like to put her in a facility. Where she can get help."

My throat constricted. "No." My voice sounded panicky and distant, even to my own ears. "No, please. Let me stay with her."

He glanced at me, and I could tell he was fighting back his sympathy for me.

Everything in me ached at the thought of Mama dying in a distant hospital, surrounded by strange faces. My desperation must have shown in my face, because Dr. Murphy's shoulders fell and he shook his head.

"If you desire, though, I can arrange for her to die at home. With nurses working around the clock, of course."

"Thank you," I breathed. "I'll take good care of her."

"Very well." Dr. Murphy paused a moment and squeezed my hand. "I'm so sorry, Alcyone."

And then he left and I was alone. Again.

* * * * *

I pressed Mama's hand against my cheek. "Mama? Mama, can you hear me?"

I dropped her wrist and pushed away from the bedside, trying to look cheerful. I crossed the room to the window. Dark curtains had been pulled. *Darn nurses.*

I could hear Mama's labored breaths from the bedside. "Of course you don't want to get up in this dreary room," I said out loud. "What was it you said? 'Waking up in the dark is never a pleasant feeling.' You said that just the other day. Remember?"

I turned. Mama's eyes were shut, her chest heaving up and down. My eyes smarted. "I wish I could catch you the sun," I whispered. I spun around and flung the curtains open. Blessed light flooded into the room. "See, Mama? It's not so dark anymore."

I ran to the fireplace and grabbed the box of matches. I scampered across the room, lighting every lamp and candle in sight. Within seconds, the room was covered in a warm glow of light.

"Allie?" she whispered. Her voice was dull and shallow.

I rushed to her side and grabbed her ashy hand. "Yes, Mama?"

"Allie … I want …" She clutched me tighter than I thought she was capable of doing. "I think … I was …" She breathed in and turned her head to the side, gasping for air.

I knelt by Mama's bedside and stroked her cheek. The lamplight illuminated the new injury on her forehead. I brushed my finger across her face, stroking the scar.

God help her. The thought came unbidden. And yet I meant it. With all my heart, I begged God to help her.

Fix her. Heal her. I'll do whatever it takes. Just please. Please don't take her from me.

Her skin grew cool and clammy as her breathing lessened.

No. My heart sank. *No, no, no.*

I turned away. "I know!" I said with false brightness. "I'll …" I struggled to choke out the words. "I'll play you a song on the piano. I've been practicing for your … birthday."

I walked over to the old piano and lifted the lid. I slid into the seat and began the cheeriest song I knew. Song after song, I played, my fingers stumbling as tears threatened to burst.

Mama had stopped breathing. I knew it, but I shoved it deep inside my chest, refusing to believe it.

My fingers began to slow as I neared the third chorus of "Turkish March." And then my shoulders fell with a bang as my arms hit the piano and I burst into tears, an unfathomable ache pulling at my heart.

August 14, 1939

Mama, I wish you'd come back. It feels like all the happy things in the world have died except for me. And I'm still here and living without them. My heart hurts, *and my head hurts, and I wish that you were here to rub it.*

Tears stung at my eyes. I stopped to hold my hand up to my mouth, fighting them back. It felt like everyone in Tennessee was waiting outside for me to start the funeral. "Such a tragedy," I'd heard them say. "For such a young, healthy woman to have that happen to her. It must have been such a burden on the girl to have a crazy mother. At least she's in a better place now."

Are you in a better place, Mama? No, I don't think you're in any place at all. Christians are the crazy ones. That's what you told me—there isn't a God. There's no one listening, no one who cares.

For some reason, that thought didn't comfort me. The idea of Mama's soul disappearing completely. It was unsettling.

I love you. I'll always love you, and I believe you loved me, too. And that makes me feel just a little bit better.

"I'm sorry."

I looked up to see Sam Carroll sticking a handful of flowers in my face. I dropped my head and stared at my black satin lap, fiercely wiping my eye.

"Allie, I said I was sorry." Sam kicked his foot on the ground, sending up a small pile of dust.

I looked up and gave him a withering look. "If you hadn't been at my house, none of this would have happened."

Sam looked taken aback. "What?"

Some of the ladies at the funeral frowned at me. I lowered my voice. "If I'd been in there with Mama, I could have saved her."

"Allie," Sam whispered, hurt in his eyes.

I refused to meet his gaze. Instead I hugged myself as tightly as my too-small black dress would let me and tried to fight the tears in my eyes.

"Well." Sam laid the flowers at my feet. "I'm still sorry." He looked up at me with the saddest blue eyes—I really was tempted to believe him for a second. Just a second.

I focused on my lap once again, and Sam shuffled off with his mother, glancing back over his shoulder at me. I avoided his eye.

"Are you Alcyone?" A stuffy old lady looked down her nose at me. I nodded and wiped my nose on my sleeve. "Oh, for goodness sake, child, use a handkerchief." The lady tutted and handed me an intricately embroidered hanky. I blew my nose and handed it back to her. "Oh." The woman grimaced and placed it back in her quilted purse. "I am Mrs. Pamela Dewsbury, from the adoption agency."

"Adoption?" I squeaked.

"Yes." Mrs. Dewsbury wrinkled her nose again and brushed a spot of dirt off the bench before she sat down beside me. "You see, Alcyone, you have no family. And so we have matched you with a compatible adult who can take care of you. I am to take you back to your home and help you pack your things so we can go straight there on the six o'clock train."

My mouth hung slightly open. Mrs. Dewsbury reached over and shut it with one finger. "That is very unsightly."

Over the car ride home, Mrs. Dewsbury explained my current situation in cold detail.

"I'm sorry to have to do this to you, but most of your belongings must be sold in order to pay for your mother's funeral arrangements. You may have noticed your mother didn't have much money." She glanced at me and tightened her lip. "You shall only bring one suitcase full of things of little worth to your new home."

"What about my cat?" My heart was racing. What would I do without Daphne?

Mrs. Dewsbury shook her head. "You may not bring the cat."

I scooted to the edge of the car and looked out the window, running my finger down the glass. "Where am I going?"

Mrs. Dewsbury glanced at me sideways. "Maine."

Maine? I crouched farther into my corner. *Oh, Mama.*

Chapter 4

After great pain, a formal feeling comes—
The Nerves sit ceremonious, like Tombs…
As Freezing persons, recollect the Snow—
First—Chill—then Stupor—then the letting go—

—Emily Dickinson

I looked around my bedroom and fought back tears. *All my things. All my precious things.* The dolls Mama had given me and the little dresses we'd sewn together. The beautiful curtains we'd picked out and the sheets we'd camped out in.

I choked on a sob as I folded the last of my few articles of clothing and placed them in my bag. There was so little room left.

Think, Allie. What will you need?

I reached over and pulled down my sketchbook and chalks from my nightstand. Then I walked over to the left wall of my room and stared at all the drawings I'd placed there. Ones of me, ones of Daphne, ones of Mama.

Ones of Mama. I reached up and peeled my favorite one off the wall, holding it to my chest and stroking my finger over Mama's face. She was dressed in her favorite feedbag dress, the one with checked tulips, standing in the garden by my roses. In her hand she cupped a butterfly, but it looked like it was going to fly away any second. The look on her face was one of anticipation and excitement. The old Mama. Before the sickness.

I put the picture in my bag along with a photograph of me and Mama. Then I walked over to the bookshelf and sighed. All our favorite books. The Brontës' stories, the Greek mythology, the poems. Then I knew which book I wanted to bring.

Mrs. Dewsbury was talking on the phone in the kitchen when I snuck downstairs. There it was in the living room. Right where I had left it the night … well, the night Mama died. *The Poems of Emily Dickinson*.

For a moment, I considered running away. To the hills, or one of the abandoned farms. Somewhere near Mama's grave, where I could still visit her and feel her presence around me. Where I wouldn't feel so alone in the world.

No. I straightened my shoulders. *No, I won't run away. I'll be strong. I'll be the woman that Mama always wanted me to be—fearless and tough.*

I looked over the room one last time before running upstairs to place the book in with my meager possessions. I zipped the bag shut and sighed at all the dolls and animals that were left. "I'm sorry," I whispered, kissing every one of them, no matter how childish it felt. "I just don't have room."

Before shutting the door to my room behind me for the last time, I said good-bye to the pictures still on the wall, and the books remaining on my shelves.

I crept across the hallway to Mama's room, still hearing Mrs. Dewsbury talking from the kitchen.

Daphne met me in the middle of the hall and purred, rubbing her head against my leg.

"Oh, Daphne," I murmured, scooping her up in my arms and burying my face in her orange fur. "Oh, I'm going to miss you so much." I set her on the ground and watched her strut back down the hallway, oblivious to my heartache.

I opened the door to Mama's room and choked back more tears.

It was as if nothing had happened. The bed was still unmade and one of the windows was open. The curtains fluttered in the breeze. A book that we had been reading was still sitting on the nightstand.

I shut the door behind me and walked over to Mama's still-open piano. My fingers ran over the keys as I tried to lock the memory in my brain. I sunk into the seat and began to play.

"Pavane for a Dead Princess." It seemed fitting. Mama *was* a princess.

I played it better than I ever had before, even after hours of practicing. Tears blinded my eyes as my fingers slid down the keys, caressing every one. *This is for you, Mama. See, I told you I'd always play for you.* I strangled down a sob.

"Alcyone."

The song ended abruptly. I looked up to see Mrs. Dewsbury frowning in the doorway, and wiped away my tears fiercely. "I was just … I was just …"

Mrs. Dewsbury gulped and for a moment I wondered if she was going to cry. But then her face calmed and she cleared her throat. "It's time to go." She spun on her heel and marched back down the stairs. Maybe showing emotion wasn't something that was listed in her job description.

I closed the piano and let my arms drop. I scooped up my bag and looked around the room. *I'll be good, Mama. I promise.*

I swallowed hard and wiped my eye. "I love you," I whispered.

Then I turned on my heel and shut the door behind me.

* * * * *

"What do you think of Maine, Alcyone?"

I looked up, startled. Mrs. Dewsbury raised an eyebrow.

I turned back to the car window and leaned my cheek against the glass. Rain dribbled down, blurring everything in the distance. "It's very ... green."

"Yes, it is." Mrs. Dewsbury repositioned her purse and leaned forward to say something to the driver.

I wiped my cheek on my sleeve and fought back a sniffle, focusing on the Maine countryside around me. It was very green. And big. *Empty.*

"Here we are!" The taxi skidded to a stop. I lurched forward and grabbed my bag. "Well? What do you think?" Mrs. Dewsbury asked.

I rolled down the window and stuck my head out, gazing up at the house.

It was very large, most likely built in the late 1800s, painted white with dozens of windows and red shutters and chimneys and sharp points. I gulped and dropped my eyes.

"Alcyone Everly, get your head back into this car this very minute! I don't need you catching cold and meeting your new mother with a red nose!"

"*Mother?*" My head shot back into the car so fast I hit it on the roof. "I don't need another mom."

"Nonsense." Mrs. Dewsbury slammed the door shut and popped open her umbrella, her heels clicking on the driveway. She opened my door and frowned. "Every girl needs a mother."

I looked up at her and gulped. "I already have a mother."

"No, you don't." She raised an eyebrow and whipped around, nearly hitting me with her leather handbag. "Come along. I'm getting drenched."

She clicked on up the driveway with her umbrella, leaving me alone to shiver in the rain with my things.

We paused at the top of the steps while Mrs. Dewsbury rang the doorbell. I could hear it sounding deep inside the house. A deep, scary sound. I clutched my carpetbag close and wished I had Daphne.

The door slowly creaked opened until the woman of the house stood before us. "Yes?"

"Mrs. Dewsbury, ma'am. With your new daughter." Mrs. Dewsbury poked me in the back, forcing me to fall into a curtsy.

"Alcyone," I muttered.

"What an interesting name," the woman said. I dared to look up, only to see her eyes staring into mine. Her voice held a soft lilt, like she was singing. I glanced back down.

"Her mother chose it, Miss Beatrice." Mrs. Dewsbury looked almost nervous.

"I see. Well, she might as well come in." The woman held the door open for me and I slipped under her arm. She flashed me a quick smile that was left unrequited.

"Very good. Now, I —" Mrs. Dewsbury stopped and looked up.

Miss Beatrice held her arm up, barring the door, and smiled. "Thank you very much, Mrs. Dewsbury, but you don't have to stay. If you could send me the paperwork in the mail, I'd appreciate it." With that, Miss Beatrice shut the door and turned to me.

I stood shivering in the foyer, half-blinded by fear.

Miss Beatrice looked me up and down. Was her gaze friendly or judging? I couldn't tell.

She gave me a brief smile and turned on her heel. "Well, come along, Alcyone. I'm so happy to have you here! This house needs some cheering up."

When I didn't move, her face dimmed a little. The sight of me standing there, dressed in black and trembling at the knees, must not have been very cheering. Neither was the glare fixed on my face.

A slight sigh escaped her lips. "Well, you might as well get to bed. There will be plenty of time for introductions and tours in the morning. It's nearly eleven o'clock already!" She cleared her throat "It's like I always say, 'Often late to bed makes a girl unfit to wed.'" She sounded a little nervous, her voice getting that sing-song quality again.

What does that have to do with anything? I kept my head down to block my tears as I followed her up the staircase and down a corridor. Miss Beatrice halted in front of a door at the end of the hall and reached into her pocket to pull out a key. With the swipe of a lock, the door was open and beckoning me to enter.

I walked in before her and placed my bags on the floor.

Miss Beatrice clicked her heels and smiled. Lighting an old-fashioned oil lamp, she sighed and said, "Yes, this will do. No one's slept in here for ages! This used to be my daughter Irene's bedroom, but she moved out a few years ago." She glanced at me. "There are dry pajamas on the back of the chair. Breakfast is served at seven fifteen. Do you like oatmeal?" I didn't respond, but she continued talking anyway, her words running together. "I've always said that punctuality is the key to vitality. I do hope you have a good night." With that, Miss Beatrice turned and walked out of the room. She paused in the doorway only a brief moment—not even long enough for me to understand the look on her face. Was it happiness? Sadness? Hope?

And then she was gone and I could hear her shoes clicking down the hallway and see the lights being turned off.

I sighed and turned around to look at the room. What could I say? It looked like a lovely space, but it felt like a lonely one. There was a little four-poster bed, a cabinet for clothing, and a sturdy, old, wooden nightstand with a rusty oil lamp on it. The only bright spot in the room was the little window in the corner, with an old-fashioned lace curtain and an attached window seat. And even that area seemed dark and foreboding, with rain dripping down the glass pane.

I gulped and wiped my nose before undressing. As I climbed into bed and blew out the lamp, I thought of poor little Daphne meowing all alone in our abandoned home with no one to feed her. And of Mama's cold, empty bedroom with no one to play her piano.

"You're a nasty, *nasty* world," I whispered to the dark.

Then I rolled over and sniffed, refusing to cry myself to sleep.

Chapter 5

A word is dead
When it is said,
Some say.
I say it just
Begins to live
That day.

—Emily Dickinson

I rolled onto my back and rubbed my face. This wasn't my bed. *Where ...*

I peeked open a single eye, then squealed, diving back under the covers. *Where am I? Was I kidnapped during the night? Where's ...*

Oh. I pulled my head out of the covers and sighed. *Maine.*

I rolled around. Hanging on the wall was a clock I hadn't seen the night before. A clock that read 7:10.

Breakfast! Miss Beatrice's words from the night before rushed through my head as I jumped out of bed and rushed over to my carpetbag.

Throwing open the bag and rummaging through it, I pulled out a faded blue feedsack dress and matching hair ribbon, then fumbled with the buttons on my nightgown while glancing at the clock.

I stumbled around the room as I pulled on the dress, running into the bed. I fell to the floor with a thud. *Ugh ...*

Presentable, I opened up the door and ventured into the hallway. Last night had been such a shock I hadn't bothered to look around, and my eyes widened at how big and grand the house was. I wandered down an impressive hallway toward the smell of food.

Miss Beatrice was waiting at the head of a long table when I reached the dining room. I froze in the doorway before giving a clumsy curtsey. "Morning," I muttered.

Miss Beatrice's mouth twitched. "Good morning, Alcyone. Though such formalities won't be necessary. This is your home now too."

"Allie," I said out of habit. My face flushed and I looked down. "Um, I like to be called Allie," I whispered, twisting my hands. *And this will never be my home.*

"It suits you," Miss Beatrice said as a small smile threatened to appear. "Now eat your breakfast before it gets cold." Her voice sounded slightly less peppy than it had the night before. I wondered if she was regretting bringing me here or if she was just tired.

"Okay." I made my way toward the table, mindful of my footsteps against the floor. I slid into the chair closest to Miss Beatrice. It was wooden, and so polished with age I nearly slid back off. I pressed my back up against it and used my toes to hold myself up as I blew on my oatmeal.

I could feel Miss Beatrice's eyes on me as I slurped. "Do you like the breakfast, Allie?"

"Yes, ma'am," I said through a mouthful of food.

Miss Beatrice nodded and looked back down at her own bowl. She was a middle-aged woman—fifty or so, perhaps—tall and very skinny, with graying hair, high cheekbones, and blue eyes covered by steel gray reading glasses. Around her mouth were small, faint laugh wrinkles. I could not tell if she smiled often, or if she had smiled often at one time.

Today she was dressed in a pale-green day dress, with white gloves and a straw hat by her place. *She must have been very pretty. When she was young.*

"Well, that should be enough. Good thing you have a healthy appetite." Miss Beatrice took off her glasses and looked at me. "Well, stand up."

Slowly, I put down my spoon and stood. I squirmed as her critical eye looked me over. "How old are you?" she asked.

"Fourteen last month."

"Fourteen. The awkward age." Miss Beatrice actually smiled. "And you've been through a lot."

That was an understatement. I looked at the floor. My body still felt numb, like everything I'd been through was a dream. It wasn't.

"Well, come along." Miss Beatrice stood and brushed off her dress, grabbing her gloves and hat. "We've a tour of the house to complete."

I walked alongside her in silence as she showed me the rooms. The foyer with its paintings of the Maine countryside, the kitchen with its cupboards of fine china, the parlor with its antique lamps. The whole house belonged in the nineteenth century, really.

"And this is the library," Miss Beatrice directed, leading me into the last room on the main level.

I stood back and stared. The library was not expansive enough a description for the thousands of leather-bound books all collected in one place, with maps and ladders and shelves. I found my hand brushing spines nearby, as if the fingers couldn't help but reach out.

"The Lovell family has always been proud of its library," Miss Beatrice was saying, "There are some particularly old artifacts in this room."

"Excuse me," I squeaked. She stopped to look at me. "Am I allowed to read these books?"

"Of course. That's what the library is for."

I looked around in wonder, biting back any outward show of joy.

"Do you enjoy reading, Allie?"

"Oh, very much so."

"Hmm." Miss Beatrice put her hands behind her back and raised an eyebrow. "Reading in a young girl is very rare these days. I can't say that I'm not glad to hear it. You know I always say that a healthy appetite for books leads to a girl with more than looks."

No, I don't know that. It was so clichéd. I held back a smirk and fidgeted instead. "Yes, ma'am."

"And now, the gardens." Miss Beatrice opened up the glass door connecting to the library and stretched out her hand for me to see.

The gardens were as beautiful as Mama's—well, they were what Mama would have had if we'd had the money. There were mostly roses: red, pink, yellow, and white, faded from the summer heat, as well as lilacs and foxgloves. The blooms and greenery at the back of the house ended at a cliff that overlooked the rocky seashore below. The smell of seawater drifted toward me, and I thought of the pictures in the old album I'd left in Tennessee.

"Maine is a fine coastal area," Miss Beatrice remarked, looking down at the waves crashing on the rocks. "Do you swim?"

"No, ma'am."

"Why not?"

"My … my father drowned, ma'am," I lied. I lowered my eyes and stepped away from the edge.

"Pish-posh. There's no reason for you not to swim."

"I'd rather not."

"Oh, well then." She pulled on her hat. "Go and get something proper to cover your head. We're going out."

What? "Where?"

Miss Beatrice snapped her gloves on and looked up. "To the store, of course. To get you some new clothes." She began to walk back toward the house.

I hurried to catch up with her as she strode in the direction of a shiny coupe. "New clothes? But mine are fine. Mama made me this dress."

"Pish-posh. Those clothes look as if they're about to fall apart! That dress is much too small." Miss Beatrice opened the car door and stopped to look me over. "And that is certainly not quality made."

I gasped. "But Mama made me this!"

"Then you may simply put it away." Miss Beatrice waved her arm as if shooing away the thought and slid into the driver's seat, beckoning for me to climb in after her.

"Was she a seamstress? Your mother, I mean?" Miss Beatrice looked behind her as she pulled out of the driveway, then shifted the car's gears and looked at me.

I didn't want to talk about Mama. Not with her, not with anyone. Other people didn't understand her, and they never would. "I don't want to talk about it," I mumbled.

Silence. I shifted. The air felt oppressive.

Miss Beatrice raised an eyebrow. "Alcyone. What an interesting name. After the Greek nymph, I suppose?"

I looked at her out of the corner of my eye. "Yes. It's also a star."

"Tragic story." Miss Beatrice's gaze didn't leave the road.

"You read Greek mythology?" I can't say I didn't ask it with a bit of attitude.

"*You* read Greek mythology?" Miss Beatrice asked, examining at me and raising her eyebrow again.

I silenced myself and looked out the window. Dozens of perfect little Victorian houses whizzed past as children played in the yard, enjoying the summer afternoon.

"You and I have something in common," Beatrice declared. "We both have creative mothers."

"Beatrice isn't a creative name."

"Isn't it?" Miss Beatrice waved at someone in a posh car. I inched away from the stranger's wondering stare. "I must assume you've never read Shakespeare's *Much Ado About Nothing*, then, Alcyone."

"Oh. 'Beatrice and Benedict' Beatrice."

"The one and only."

"Interesting," I muttered.

"Well, here we are." Miss Beatrice pulled up in front of Brown's Department Store. "After you, Allie."

I slid out of the car and crossed my arms as Miss Beatrice locked the doors.

"Miss Lovell," the store clerk gushed as we entered the store. I looked around and gulped. Brown's was certainly the poshist store I'd ever been in. The mannequins were dressed in Lanvin and lace, things I'd only thought existed in fashion magazines and movie reels. It all felt rather extravagant and rich for a time when most people could barely afford to eat.

Words cannot adequately describe how awkward I felt as the store clerk led me toward the children's department. I could feel my dirty hair, see my grubby clothes. "She needs new everything," Miss Beatrice directed, looking around. "A church dress, a party dress, six or seven school dresses, underthings, nightgowns, hats, gloves, and, of course, footwear." They both eyed my clunky brown shoes. I bit my lip and looked down. "I believe she can wait on a coat and winter gloves a few more months. What do you think, Isla?"

"Definitely." Isla smiled as she took my measurements. Her powder blue dress was *definitely* too tight.

"And what do you think for her coloring?" Miss Beatrice asked. "I was debating between pale green — for her eyes — royal blue, and lavender. And of course girls always look good in pink." She sighed. "I've always said that pink embodies the wink of girlhood."

"I don't like pink." I wrinkled my nose.

"No pink!" Isla chirped, disappearing into the back of the store.

"White is always a good choice too," Miss Beatrice murmured to herself. "For girls."

"How are these?" Isla asked—happily—as she returned with a pile of clothes.

"Perfect," Miss Beatrice said, delighted with the frothy things Isla had fetched.

Ugh.

In the end, we left the store with a white church dress, an emerald green party dress, assorted school clothes in gray, brown, and red, three checkered rompers, two nightgowns, as well as half a dozen underthings, hats, and white gloves.

I climbed into the car in a new peach dress Isla had proclaimed perfect for my skin tone, half exhausted, just as my stomach let out a loud grumble.

Miss Beatrice looked at me. I could tell she was fighting back a smile. "Hungry, Allie?"

"Yes, ma'am," I mumbled.

"Thought so. Might as well go to Goodey's." She started the engine and pulled out of the department store. I thought I saw the overly perky sales clerk waving from a window and shuddered.

"You'll like Goodey's," Miss Beatrice continued. "It's one of the most comfortable joints in town."

Maine looked so much different in the dry daylight. It was sort of cute—all the buildings so small and quaint. We passed by the grocers, the post office, the cinemas, and dozens of little stores before we got to what I had to assume was the comfortable joint in question.

We pulled up in the parking lot beside a little pink automobile. I couldn't help it—my eyebrows raised and I reached out for Miss Beatrice. She turned in alarm. "What is it?"

I pointed. "That car is *pink*!" *Who ever thought of such a thing?*

Miss Beatrice smiled as if I were some flighty child. "Yes, that's Irene Goodey's car. She's an ... *interesting* young woman." She began to open the door, then turned to look at me. "You'll see plenty of that pink car in the future, Allie. Come on."

I looked over my shoulder one last time before walking into the restaurant with Miss Beatrice.

Someone squealed upon our entrance.

What in the world? I looked up to see a woman in a hot pink dress come running in our direction, hands outreached. *I didn't know they made fabric in that color.*

"Irene," Miss Beatrice said, holding out her arms. The two embraced, and from my spot I could just catch a whiff of the perfume Irene was wearing.

"Oh, and *who* is *this*?" Irene asked, turning to me. She was young, maybe twenty or so, with bright red hair and green eyes. She gave me a dazzling smile, and for a moment I forgot that she talked in accented syllables and wore hot pink. She was that pretty.

"This is Al-cee-u-nee." Beatrice drew out every syllable.

Irene wrinkled her little nose, amused. "I'm going to have to get you to write that one down."

"Call me Allie." I was stricken with a sudden shyness that caused me to look down at my shiny new shoes.

Irene grinned. "*I'm* Irene. And I just know I'm going to love you." She winked at me. "After all, we're sisters now."

Sisters? My brows pinched together. *But that would mean . . .*

Miss Beatrice smiled and turned to me. "Alcyone, this is Irene Goodey, my daughter."

Irene grinned and squeezed Miss Beatrice's spidery hand, then giggled. "Don't let her get the better of you, cheeky. Stick up for yourself and she'll never spank you *too* hard."

Miss Beatrice frowned at Irene and dropped her hand. But there was a twinkling in her eye. "Irene Goodey! Speaking like that to a child! I ought to spank you right now."

I found myself breathing a prayer — something I never do — out to the universe for poor Miss Goodey's safety. However, my prayers didn't need much answering, because the next second Irene was laughing and pouring us both tall glasses of iced tea.

"How do you like my restaurant, darling?" Irene asked, sending me a wink.

I looked around the room. The tiled floors were squeaky clean, the tables neat and tidy, the soda machines shiny and new. The whole place could have been a spread out of Mama's *Good Housekeeping* magazine, were it not for the splashes of pink. Just where you thought there wouldn't be, a patch of hot pink would flash at you from some discreet corner. The menus, the roses on the tables, the fuchsia-colored clock.

I frowned. Honestly, pink was following me everywhere.

I turned to Irene as realization dawned on me. "You own this restaurant."

Irene stared at me in silence before throwing back her head and laughing — a half choking, half snorting sound that was utterly charming and unpredictable. I ducked my head again.

"Why, *honey*," Irene chuckled, glancing at Beatrice, "you didn't realize that?"

Even Miss Beatrice couldn't resist a smile. "It is called Goodey's Diner, Alcyone."

"I can't take all the credit for it, though." Irene grinned at Beatrice. "Mom gave Daniel and me the money to start it."

I risked a sideways glance at Miss Beatrice and took a long sip of my tea. She gave Irene a warm smile and then sent it in my direction.

As if I needed her smiles. Or her love. As if I would ever be part of her big, happy "family."

A knot formed in my stomach and I looked away. All of a sudden I felt tired and lonely and homesick. And empty.

* * * * *

"I don't want to go to church."

Miss Beatrice's eyes widened. "Why not?"

I stuck my chin out and looked away. "Mama says church is for superstitious fools who don't have enough guts to stand on their own two feet."

Miss Beatrice put down the pretty white dress and bit her lip. "I see." She sat down in the armchair and folded her hands in her lap, as if trying to think of what to do. "Allie," she finally said, "faith isn't about superstition or leaning on others because you haven't got any ... guts. It takes guts to believe sometimes. To know that even when things don't look like they're going well, God is still there and he's still guiding you. Faith like

72

that—the faith to trust Christ enough to take the place for your sins and take control of your life. Faith like that takes all the guts in the world. And it's worth it. Do you believe me?"

I squirmed under her gaze and refused to answer. "There is no God," I muttered.

As if shocked by a powerful current, Miss Beatrice stood and crossed over to the window. She pulled back the deep-red curtains and let the sunlight pierce the room.

I squinted as my eyes strained to adjust. Outside the window, a thick green vine hugged the glass, and on its end a small purple morning glory lifted its face toward the sun.

After opening the window, Miss Beatrice reached out and fingered the flower. "Allie, if there is no God, who do you think made the flowers? Who do you think made you?"

I focused on the wall to her left. "It doesn't matter because I'm in charge of myself. No God is going to rule me." I swallowed the lump in my throat and lifted my chin.

She sighed and shut the window. "I will be going to church, if you wish to come with me."

I bit the inside of my cheek. "No, thank you."

"Very well. I won't make you." Miss Beatrice paused in the doorway. "I don't mind you staying home alone for an hour, if you promise to behave."

"I promise."

"Very well." Her mouth twitched. "But I have always said that—"

"Why do you do that?"

She blinked slowly, clearly unused to being interrupted. "Do what?"

I swung my legs and crossed them under my little chair. "You start many of your statements with, 'I always say …'" I tilted my head. "I was just wondering why."

In a way I never would have expected of an older woman, Miss Beatrice rolled her eyes and opened the door. A smile played around on her lips. "I always say a child should never question an adult."

"That one didn't rhyme," I pointed out.

She grinned and shut the door.

Chapter 6

I measure every grief I meet
With analyctic eyes;
And wonder if it weighs like mine,
Or has an easier size.

—Emily Dickinson

The house seemed even bigger and emptier when I was the only living thing in it. I walked around the kitchen, taking the time to study everything while no one could see me.

My stomach grumbled, leading me to the icebox. The amount of food took me aback: there was milk and eggs and fruit and anything else you could want. I reached for a jar of pickles, then halted. *This is Miss Beatrice's food, not mine.*

I shut the icebox firmly and made my way into the library. My pace slowed as I examined the titles. *The Travels of Marco Polo ... Alice in Wonderland ... The Adventures of Robin Hood ... Ivanhoe ...*

Miss Beatrice must have quite the imagination.

I settled on a worn copy of *A Little Princess* and sat down in a little chair by the window, so I could look out and see the roses.

As I flipped through the book's pages, memories flooded back over me of reading by the fireplace with Mama. I could still see her face, concentrated on her knitting, helping me as I stumbled over the harder words.

Shutting the book with a thud, I slipped it back on the shelf and left the library.

* * * * *

"I assure you, no one will stare," Miss Beatrice said.

I glanced at her uncertainly out of the corner of my eye.

"It's just a schoolyard, Alcyone. They're just children."

I looked out the window at the dozens of boys and girls, dressed in clean, pressed dresses and slacks, running up to the doorstep of the school.

I gulped. "I don't know if I can do this."

"Pish-posh." Miss Beatrice reached over and opened up my door. She bent her forehead until her eyes were only a few inches from mine. "You can and you will do this, Alcyone."

As soon as she turned to climb out of the car, I sent a fierce scowl at her back, feeling a little better.

I reached down to smooth my burgundy school dress, glancing about as Beatrice marched up the school steps. A few of the children stopped to stare at me.

The principal's office was obsessively clean. White-washed walls, scratch-free floors, stainless desks. I squirmed and ducked behind Beatrice, and was immediately mad at myself for doing so.

"Can I help you?" the secretary sighed, looking at us from behind her silver-framed glasses. She twisted her piece of pink gum around her finger.

"Yes," Miss Beatrice said, motioning to me with a grand air. "This is Alcyone Lovell."

"Alcyone *Everly*," I interrupted.

My correction fell on deaf ears. "I've come to enroll her in the ninth grade."

The secretary stared at me for what seemed like a whole minute before drawling, "I see. And how do you spell that?"

Suddenly, the door burst open and a pretty blonde girl flew in. Her golden curls, tousled from the activity, whipped around behind her as she stuck her tongue out at a grinning boy and stamped her foot. "You stay away from me, Andy Brown, ya hear?" With a regal air, she turned and rolled her eyes at the secretary. "He just will not leave me alone!" With a fluid motion she straightened and smiled at me. "Hi, I'm Charlie, who are you?" A slight Southern accent made the words float across the air. "Where're you from? Are you just visiting or staying forever?" She tilted her head. "Have I seen you before?"

I must have looked like a total fool as I stood there and stared at her, because after a moment she wrinkled her nose and turned to the lady behind the desk. "Miss Mary, what's wrong with this girl?"

Mary sighed again and pushed up her glasses. "Dunno. She still hasn't given me her name."

Miss Beatrice leaned forward and pointed at Mary's book. "A-l-c-y-o-n-e."

The girl turned toward me again and beamed, flipping a

stray curl off her shoulder. "I'm Charlie Cooper. My daddy's the principal here. As of last year, at least."

"Charlie? Isn't that a boy's name?" *Great, now I've probably offended her.*

Charlie snorted and threw back her curls. "Oh, no, not at all. My real name's Charlotte, but when I was young the boys took to callin' me Charlie, and it stuck."

"The boys?"

"My brothers. I've got five of them," Charlie said proudly, sticking up her palm. "Now what's your name?" She peeked over Miss Beatrice's shoulder at the sheet. "Al-ki-o-nee?"

"You say it *Al-cee-u-nee*." I paused. "But I like Allie. Allie Everly."

"Oh." Charlie looked me up and down for a second. "I like you, Allie," she said suddenly. "You've got beautiful eyes. I just know we're gonna be best friends."

I looked down as I felt my cheeks heat. *Beautiful eyes?* They were just a light bluish-green. And I had plain, dark hair too. Not straight enough to hang loose and not curly enough to fluff; just sort of blackish-brown, wavy hair, rather than a gorgeous, golden halo like Charlie's. And my freckles! Four under my right eye and five under my left! Talk about misfortune.

"I just know you're going to love this school," Charlie was saying—no, gushing—as she looped her arm in mine. She opened the door and let me pass through first. "I'll show Allie to her class," she called behind her as she led me down the hall.

I smiled and hugged my books to my chest. Boys were watching us discreetly as we made our way straight down the center. I glanced at Charlie and realized she was sort of strutting down the hallway. If I tried to copy her gait, would I look like an actress or a waddling duck? I decided not to risk it.

"Why's everyone looking at us?" I whispered.

Charlie looked around and for the first time seemed to recognize everyone around her. "Oh, don't mind them," she whispered back. "They always do that. You don't realize it after a while, though." She squeezed my arm. "Say, did you know I met FDR? Yeah, I was on summer vacation and ..."

I held my head up high as I walked to my class. My *friend* was with me now.

* * * * *

The window seat of my new bedroom was the perfect place to look out over the ocean. In my hands I clutched a stuffed animal I'd found on the bed. It was a cute little bear, with button eyes and a brown nose. It looked homemade, which was probably the reason I chose it.

I looked back down at the notebook in front of me.

September 19, 1939

The sky is alive tonight, Mama. With thousands of sparkling stars. Usually they're grand and silent, but tonight they're feisty and bold. The last one on the Big Dipper keeps winking at me!

I let out a deep breath and looked back up at the sky. Can you see stars in heaven?

I know you said heaven doesn't exist, Mama, but I wish I knew where you were right now. I heard a little girl once say that her baby sister died and became a star. Are you a star now, Mama, smiling down on me? Or are you just darkness, floating around in space? You know, you never told me what happens after death. I suppose it's silly of me to think anything does.

I paused and looked over what I'd written. It didn't seem appropriate, so I ripped it out and started over.

I made a friend today. Her name is Charlie Cooper and she's funny and pretty and nice. And I have Miss Beatrice Lovell too, who is sometimes awful and sometimes sort of okay. Sometimes I think I can't tell the difference anymore. I wish you were here to help me.

I groaned softly and closed the notebook with a slam, biting my lip.

Someone knocked on the door. I looked up to see Miss Beatrice standing in the doorway, in good spirits. Her hair was down and around her white-robed shoulders.

"I see you found my teddy bear."

I nodded and let go of the bear a little bit.

"His name is Mr. Bearington."

I hid my smile deep down inside and frowned. "That's a silly name."

Miss Beatrice nodded and leaned in the doorway, watching me. "I haven't seen him in ages. I was afraid he was gone forever." She crossed the room and sat across from me on the window seat. I scooted away. "Isn't that moon something?" she asked. "I watched it from this room when I was a little girl. And yet it never changes." She looked down and rubbed the material of her robe almost nervously. "Allie, I'm sorry. I know how hard this has been for you. A new life, a new family."

She turned and looked me in the eye. A cheery smile spread over her face. "But we'll get through this together." I didn't breathe as she reached over and tucked a piece of hair behind my ear, her eyes softening. "Allie." Her hand lingered around my jaw. "I've always wanted another daughter."

My breath left my lungs so quickly all I could do was recoil, banging my head against the wall. "I'll *never* be your daughter."

Miss Beatrice dropped her hand as if she'd been slapped. I thought I saw hurt and loneliness flash across her face, but then it was empty again.

Without another word, the door shut and I was alone.

I opened up my journal again and began to scribble fiercely, my tears making the page seem blurry.

Why did you leave me, Mama? Why? Why did you leave me by myself?

I made a strangled sobbing sound, looking away. The moon was still shining, but now it seemed distant — almost like it was retreating from my view. I rubbed my hand across my eye and ripped out the page again.

I promise not to cry too much, Mama. I promise I'll be good. I'll never forget you, no matter what Miss Beatrice says. She'll never be my mama. I won't let you down. I promise.

Until we meet again,

Your Allie

I slammed the journal shut and put a hand over my mouth to muffle the tears. I looked down. Mr. Bearington was still in my other hand.

"Stupid bear!" I screamed, throwing it across the room. Then I collapsed against the window in tears, the glass cold against my sore, throbbing head.

"Oh, Mama," I whispered into my arm, "I just want to go home."

Part Two

1943–1945

Chapter 7

A narrow fellow in the grass
Occasionally rides;
You may have met him,——did you not,
His notice sudden is.

—Emily Dickinson

What are you reading?"

I looked up to see Beatrice grimacing at me from across the table. *Why should I bother telling her it's Emily Dickinson?* I broke our eye contact and turned the page.

Beatrice buttered a piece of toast. The clinking of her knife pierced the silent air. "I have to make sure our dresses are pressed for this afternoon. I'll wear the green one and you will be wearing the new blue one." Without even bothering to look at me squarely, she said, "Don't make that face, Allie. Russell will think the blue one lovely."

I put the book down just long enough to take a sip of milk. Natural light flooded the sunroom, casting shadows on my page.

"And our nylons have to be steamed too." Beatrice frowned to herself.

The silence filled the table. For as long as I'd lived here, it had been like this. Awkward silence. Stilted conversation. Beatrice always reaching to pull something out of me that I wasn't willing to give.

Beatrice took a last bite of toast. "You know what? I think I'm going to go get ready. Finish up, Allie. The party begins at one."

She walked out of the dining room muttering, finally leaving me alone. I sighed and opened up Dickinson again.

My eyes skimmed the page, but none of the words sank in.

* * * *

Gosh, could life be any more boring?

"And boom! We blasted their heads off!"

Laughter erupted among the group. I looked around to see Beatrice nodding as Debra Wilkinson gripped her arm. I forced a smile and went back to counting the blades of grass under my shoes. I held my notebook firmly behind my back so no one would take notice. Every fiber of my being longed to be giggling and talking with Charlie instead of being forced to play good society girl at this stupid party.

Humphrey Wilkinson laughed and rubbed his stomach. "Well," he bellowed, "I said to myself, 'Humphrey Wilkinson, you've done your job, killed your Germans, and soon you'll win your war. Then you can go home and teach your good ol' son to do the same.'" He patted Russell on the back.

"Papa," Russell moaned, blushing like a little girl.

This time I smiled for real. *"Papa"? Oh, please.*

Russell glanced at me and grinned. "As soon as I marry I'll get up and go join the war in Europe myself. Yes, sir, I will."

My happy feelings vanished and I dropped my gaze back to the ground. *I wish they'd draft you now.* I winced. *That was a cruel thought.*

Humphrey's booming laughter filled the lawn again. "That's my boy!"

A late May breeze tickled my neck. For as far as I could see, prissy young ladies and prissy old ladies and prissy middle-aged ladies paraded about as obnoxious men laughed much too loudly. *What a wearisome day.*

Debra leaned toward Beatrice and spoke just loud enough for me to hear. "Russell's always wanted to join the army. Ever since he was a boy, in fact. But his father and I told him he needed to find a wife first." She smiled and checked to see if I was listening. "Tell me, Beatrice, has Allie had any boyfriends lately? Any young suitors crawling around at your place?" She winked.

Oh, that does it! Really, do these people have no discretion? I sent visual daggers toward her back.

"No," Beatrice said, sipping her lemonade. "She claims she's too sensible for romance."

I had to do something to stop this. Before long, they'd be choosing my wedding dress and discussing names for my children.

"Beatrice?" I tapped her on the shoulder.

"Yes?" She turned around, annoyed.

I put on my sweetest face and rubbed my forehead. "May I please be excused? I have a terrible headache."

"Of course. Just don't wander far."

I nodded and turned on my heel. I could hear them all laughing again at something—Humphrey's booming voice covering all the others'. I took a final glance at the white mansion on the hill and shuddered.

"Allie!"

Someone grabbed my arm. I jumped and whipped around, practically knocking into Russell. I rolled my eyes and pulled my arm away, relieved. "Oh, Russell, you scared me! Could you come with a warning bell or something? I'd like to know when *you're* behind me." I tried to turn, but Russell reached out and touched my arm, startling me in a whole new way.

Russell wrung his pale, white hands. "I'd like to think I won't soon need to be telling you. I mean, I'll still be needing to tell you, but maybe soon you won't need to be told or you won't … Oh, Allie, was I being too presumptuous?" He reached out and grabbed my arm again.

What? I stared at him for a moment, wondering what bad drama he'd seen at the theater last Friday. "By asking to follow me around?"

He smiled and shook his head. "No, my love. By making my intentions clear in front of everyone." He tightened his grip on my arm, his small eyes crinkling in a poor imitation of a lover.

A woman walked by and raised her eyebrow at us.

"Russell!" I leaped back, tearing myself from his grasp. I resisted the urge to wipe my arm against my dress. "Russell, I have to tell you—"

"No!" Suddenly Russell's finger was pressed against my lip, silencing me. My eyes widened and I stared at him in silence, too afraid to move. "Let me be the first to speak," Russell cried. I gulped. People were beginning to stare.

"I mean to marry you, Allie," Russell proclaimed. "I mean for you to marry me. I mean for us to be husband and wife. To be a family. I mean for—"

"I don't want to marry you, Russell!" I slapped his hand away and took a step back, very much disturbed, though I tried to look relaxed and pleasant. "Enjoy the party."

I pivoted and practically ran away from him, conscious of the crowd now gathering to watch the spat. Why was my life so complicated?

When I chanced a look back, Russell was shrugging. "She doesn't want to rush things," I thought I heard him say.

I shuddered. *He is a creep. Or incredibly dense.*

* * * * *

"Oh, Allie, there you are. Come here." Beatrice motioned toward me, acting as if she hadn't seen me in years. "I want you to say hello to Miss Rachel."

Great. Brushing off my skirt, I trudged over to the table where Beatrice and Miss Rachel were sitting. "Good afternoon."

Rachel Piper smiled slowly, revealing two rows of even teeth. Then she sighed and patted her gray pompadour. "How are you, Alcyone?"

"Just fine, thank you." The back of my leg itched. I lifted a foot to scratch it, careful not to let anyone see. Beatrice especially wouldn't let me hear the end of it—she'd been trying for years to get me to act "proper." As I checked to make sure my actions had stayed discreet, my eyes met with a young man sitting across the garden. He smiled at me, his blue eyes crinkling.

How *do* I even know they were blue? I'd never seen him before.

Beatrice touched my arm and smiled. "Rachel was just telling me about the delightful garden party she held last weekend. Would you like to hear, Allie?"

I fought a grimace. "No, thanks."

Miss Rachel raised a pointed eyebrow. "I see," she said, pursing her lip. "Tell me, Alcyone: have you met my nephew, Samuel? He's staying with me for the summer."

I shook my head. "Sorry." *Oh no. Now I'm going to have to stand here for another half hour and listen to her praise her precious nephew.* But something niggled in the back of my mind.

Miss Rachel raised a gloved hand and waved it. "Samuel! Come over here!" She grabbed my hand, as if afraid I would leave the table at any moment. "You must meet your neighbor."

I turned and saw the young man across the garden rise and make his way toward us. Up close, I could tell I was right about his eyes. My head felt pinched. *How ... how do I know his face?*

"Hello," he said, extending a hand to Beatrice. "I'm Samuel."

"Pleased to meet you. I've always said that a new friend is a journey on life's fresh bend." Beatrice smiled and turned to say something to Miss Rachel.

Samuel raised an eyebrow before turning and sticking out his hand. "And your name is?"

I stared at him in silence. *His face ... his hair ... his eyes ... What's wrong with me?* My brain felt fuzzy. *Maybe I'm getting a tumor!* I gulped, feeling panicked. *What are the first signs?*

"I'm sorry, could you say that again?"

I jerked to attention, nearly knocking Samuel's arm. He had a wry smile on his lips, obviously enjoying my discomfort. "Allie," I said, avoiding his hand.

He chuckled and pulled his arm back in. "And, um, are you okay, Allie?"

"Yes. I'm fine." I looked around. *An escape. I need an escape.* "I, uh … I have to go." I spun on my heel and ran down toward the beach, clutching my notebook to my chest.

* * * * *

The cold waves lapped against my bare toes. I wiggled them in the sand and smiled to myself. Resituating myself on the rock, I held my drawing away from me and studied it. From the safety of shore, I could still hear people enjoying the party.

Russell's nose isn't quite that big. I bit my lip and erased the nose. With a few quick lines, the problem was solved.

I looked down at the page again. Maybe a picture of Russell wasn't quite appropriate next to a page containing a lovely poem about the moon. But it had to fit somewhere. I would not survive this day if I couldn't take out all my frustration into a horrid drawing of Russell as *I* saw him.

"Who's that?"

I jumped and looked up. I could just make out a man's figure from behind my curtain of dark hair. Since when did my hair come loose?

I pushed the hair aside and saw Samuel standing in front of me. One dark eyebrow was cocked, his mouth crinkling in amusement.

I glanced down at the caricature and blushed. It certainly wasn't the most polite portrait to be caught drawing.

The young man was still smirking. I noticed his trousers were rolled up and his brown hair was tousled from the wind.

I finally spoke. "Wh-what?"

"I said, 'Who's that?'" He pointed at the portrait.

"No one. No one at all." I tilted the notebook away from him and tried to scare him off with a withering glare.

He just smiled and leaned close enough to look over my shoulder. "Doesn't look like no one. Looks to me like an ugly rich boy. Your boyfriend?"

I snapped the notebook shut and snorted. "No, thank goodness."

"Then your sister's boyfriend."

"No."

"Hmmm ..." He began strolling down the shore. I saw he was barefoot too. "I've got it!" He snapped his fingers and grinned. "Your brother! No, your cousin?"

I let my mouth raise a little. "Try again."

Samuel studied me. "Could he be the reason you left the party? An unwanted suitor perhaps?"

My eyebrows flew up. I hid my smile and smoothed out my skirts. "No, actually his name was Rumpelstiltskin, but I knew you'd never guess it."

The boy smiled, his blue eyes crinkling. "It was on the tip of my tongue."

I doubted that. "Sure it was."

He swept into an elegant bow. "Honest, my lady," he said, grinning.

I rolled my eyes and opened up my notebook again, continuing my sketch of Russell. This time I threw in a few extra touches to make him as prissy as possible.

"Unfortunately for you, I learned in princess school never to trust the word of a stranger. Especially not bareheaded, shoeless, beach-roaming vagabonds. So I'm afraid you're out of luck." Even as the words flew out of my mouth, I couldn't believe it was me saying them. My tone was full of arrogance and rudeness, but could it also be interpreted as inviting? My cheeks flushed. I hoped not.

"Well then, I shall just have to prove my innocence to you another way." He motioned to the ocean. "A swimming contest, perhaps?"

I looked down, straightening my back. "No, actually I don't swim. Especially not with *strangers*."

"Don't or can't?"

I hated that he was challenging me. "Can't."

He smirked. "Now's a perfect time to learn."

The book was slammed shut again. "Are you crazy? I don't have a swimsuit."

"Neither do I."

"The water's probably freezing." *Who was this ridiculous ...*

"Only one way to find out."

I looked up, frustrated, and caught a mischievous gleam in his eye. He was daring me. "I don't even know you," I said. The challenge lingered in the air, taunting me. I knew I shouldn't, but I was too stubborn to resist.

I followed him to the edge of the water and dipped my toe in. I was right—It was cold. "Beatrice will kill me."

He raised an eyebrow, and I knew I had to do it. I shut my eyes and took a step into the water, wincing when the water reached my knees and caused my dress to cling to my legs. I opened my eyes and looked at him.

He looked pleased. "Just like that. Nice and easy. It's not so bad, is it?"

I scowled at him. "I've hardly reached my knees."

"You're almost halfway there."

I frowned at him and his silly, roguish smile. Goosebumps popped up on my legs. I held my skirts tight. "I'm not getting in any farther. I can't go back to the party wet. I'm just going to go back."

I started to turn around and make my way back to the sand.

"Allie!" Samuel suddenly shouted. "Get b——" And then his voice was muffled by the gurgling sound of rushing water.

A wave crashed on my back, whipping my feet out from under me. I let out a gurgled scream as my world turned to freezing, swirling blackness. I flailed in the water, tried to stand, and fell back down. "Oh no." My voice came out panicky and waterlogged. "Oh, dear heavens. Oh my word."

Samuel came up laughing, water sputtering out of his mouth. He shook his head, droplets flying.

I stood and twisted my skirt back into place as the water retreated back into the ocean. I pushed the hair out of my face, and noticed sand covered my backside. Beatrice would die when she saw me.

Just after the thought drifted though my mind, voices floated from the direction of the party. Someone was coming this way.

I groaned and waded back to shore, muttering under my breath.

"Allie!" Samuel shook his hair again and tried to run after me, the water slowing him down. "Are you okay? Did you get water up your nose or something?" He grabbed my shoulder and attempted to turn me toward him.

Heat seeped through my body. I whipped around and pushed him hard in the chest. "That's for making me get in the water," I spat.

He flailed and fell backward, his hand still on my shoulder. I tumbled with him, back into the ice-cold water.

This time we both came up at the same time, sputtering for air.

"I'm sorry, Allie," Samuel was saying, trying to pull me up out of the water. For a few seconds we were caught in a strange balancing act as we both attempted to climb to our feet. "I'm so sorry."

And then it hit me. "Sam Carroll?" I steadied myself and took a step back. Time stood still as the years came rushing back over me.

Sam looked nervous. He licked his lips and nodded. "Yeah."

I stared at him in silence. It made sense. The blue eyes. The dark hair. The way he watched me and teased me and smiled at me. The fact that I didn't really hate him, despite the fact he nearly drowned me.

I took another step back, aware all over again of how wet and dirty I was. "What are you doing here?"

How did he find me? After all these years? I wasn't sure whether to be angry or happy. Surprised, yes. Even a little scared.

Sam kicked a little splash in the water. "My aunt Rachel lives here. So I thought I'd visit for the summer."

"Did you know I was here?"

"Well, yeah." Sam looked up and caught my gaze, looking both embarrassed and amused. "I mean, Aunt Rachel mentioned you were her neighbor. And that she'd seen you."

I blinked. "But I didn't know about you."

"Oh. Sorry." Sam smiled slowly.

Just like his aunt to spring this on me. I shivered. How could I not have seen it?

"Allie?" I looked up to see Beatrice standing on the shore, staring at us with a mixture of shock and concern.

I jumped away from Sam and tried to peel my soaking-wet dress away from my body. "Oh my gosh, I'm so sorry ..." I stumbled, my face heating up. "This is ... um ..."

"Samuel." Beatrice's mouth twitched. "We met a few minutes ago, remember?"

Of course it's Sam Carroll. I tried to compose myself. "Yes, Sam. We were swimming. In the ocean. It's not bad, actually. A little ... wet ... but ... not bad." I bit my lip and half-swam, half-waded to shore.

"You were laughing."

"What?" I looked at Beatrice. Was everyone going crazy?

"I heard laughter, so I came to see what was happening. You were snorting water out of your nose." She seemed strangely calm.

I reached up to smooth down my hair and attempted to look composed. "Yes, well ... Sam was just ..."

Beatrice smiled at Sam and shook his hand more warmly. "It's been a pleasure meeting you, Sam. I do hope we'll see you again this summer."

I pulled on my shoes and grabbed my notebook. This was just way too awkward. I flopped my hat on top of my dripping head and trudged back up the hill toward the party.

Beatrice went on to exclaim, "To think you'll be living practically next door to us! Allie, this is wonderful! Allie?" She raised her voice as I got closer to the festivities. "Allie! Allie, don't you dare go back there looking like that!" I turned to see her looking back at Sam. "Do come for supper one night. And tell your aunt I said good-bye." Then she ran after me, practically yelling, "Allie! Allie, come back here!"

Chapter 8

The moon was but a chin of gold
A night or two ago,
And now she turns her perfect face
Upon the earth below.

—Emily Dickinson

I could still feel my cheeks burning as Beatrice drove in silence. Sam Carroll. I had never been so humiliated in my life. Why, I bet he knew who I was the whole time and was just toying with me as revenge for how I used to treat him.

I pulled the blanket around me closer. And after that last thing I said to him too. I basically accused him of my mother's death by saying she'd still be alive if he wasn't there.

Shame at those words seeped over me. *Ugh, I could just die right now.*

"You didn't have to be so rude," Beatrice said. "All I said was that he made you laugh. No one makes you laugh. You can't blame me for pointing it out."

I sighed. "That was Sam."

"I know. And he's staying with his aunt Rachel for the summer. I was listening, you know."

I groaned and leaned my cheek against the car window. "No, no, Beatrice, that was *Sam*. Sam *Carroll*. I grew up with him."

"And you just stood there bumbling while the poor boy was forced to introduce himself like a complete stranger?" Beatrice's eyebrows shot up.

"I hadn't seen him since the funeral. I didn't recognize him, so he *was* a complete stranger." I sighed. I was such a fool.

Beatrice glanced over at me. "So did he recognize you?"

I groaned. "I don't want to talk about it."

"Okay, okay. Sorry." Beatrice tapped the steering wheel for a few seconds. "So was he a mean kid?"

"No, he just ... He wasn't mean. He was nice." I snuggled into the blanket. "And smart. He was just ..." I trailed off again. He was just Sam. I turned to Beatrice and chewed my lip. "He came from a perfect home, you know? It was like he had everything he'd ever need." I grimaced "He followed me around everywhere."

"So you were friends."

"No, I ... It was nothing." Why did I think she'd understand? Why did I think anyone would understand my complicated life?

I could tell Beatrice had more questions by the way she looked at me, but she remained quiet for the rest of the car ride.

✷ ✶ ✷ ✶ ✷

"Beatrice!" I shouted, grabbing a light sweater from the coatrack by the door. "I'm going out for a soda. Be back in an hour!" I slammed the door behind me and climbed into Beatrice's car, humming to myself.

I pulled out of the driveway as I heard Beatrice calling from the steps. *She won't mind if I only take it for a little hour-long ride.* I resisted the urge to look behind me.

I slid into the Goodey's parking lot and turned off the engine. Charlie's car was parked beside me, which meant it was going to be a good day.

"Hey, girl!" Charlie shouted as I entered the diner. She held up a soda and winked. "Are you here for a drink?"

I rolled my eyes and smiled at the boy behind the counter. "I'll take a Coke, please."

Charlie took a sip of her soft drink and clicked her glass with her long pink fingernails.

The bell over the door rang, signaling more customers. I turned to see a group of kids from school laughing and joking with each other. They noticed us and waved. "Hey, Allie!" one of the boys shouted, "How many more days of school?"

"You'll never get me to engage in conversation with you, Danny Parker!" I called back, flicking my hair.

"Ouch." Charlie laughed and nudged me.

I gave her a dismissive look. "He deserved it. He's been bothering me ever since ninth grade."

Charlie took another sip of her soda. "So are you an elitist now?"

"If I am, I got it from you."

Charlie nodded and kicked the counter with her new shoes. "You know what?"

"What?" I grabbed my soda from the soda jerk, mumbling a quick thanks.

"One day you're going to find a boy who really cares about you, and who you really care about too. Then your elitism is going to get you in trouble."

I rolled my eyes, fidgeting on the end of my chair. "Is this about Russell?"

Charlie held up her hands. "Hey, you mentioned him. Not me."

"Because Russell is not my type."

She arched an eyebrow. "I didn't know you had a type." A slow smile spread across her face as she fiddled with her straw.

My face flushed. "I don't." Sam's face flashed across my mind, causing me to blush all over again. "I definitely don't," I said again, more forcefully this time.

"Ooookay." Charlie drew out the word, making it sound anything but okay.

This topic was getting uncomfortable. I glanced around the room. My eyes fell on the new jukebox. "Hey!" I called to the soda jerk boy. "Does that thing work?"

The boy shrugged. "Think so."

"Have any good records?" Charlie asked. She twirled a blonde curl around her finger and grinned, revealing her two rows of straight teeth.

The boy squirmed and looked down, grabbing a dish towel. "Um, I think there's some Benny Goodman and Bing Crosby records over there."

I wrinkled my nose. "Crosby's for old people and mothers. Why don't you play some Benny Goodman?"

Charlie giggled and nodded. "I agree."

"Sure." The boy took off his apron and knelt by the shiny jukebox. He slid in a few coins and pressed a button. Within seconds, the orchestra started up and the sounds of Benny Goodman floated into the air.

The rest of the noise in the diner dimmed to a hush. The kids began to whisper and nudge each other.

"What song is this?" I asked.

Charlie looked at the album and smiled. "Conchita, Marquita, Lolita, Pepita, Rosita, Juanita Lopez."

I raised an eyebrow and watched the jukebox. "It's nice."

When the song finished, I handed the fountain boy a nickel. "Thanks for the soda." I slid out of the chair.

"Oh, wait!"

I turned to see him holding up a glass jar. "For the war effort."

I nodded and pulled out a quarter. "For the war effort." Then I turned and smiled at Charlie. "I've got to get going before Beatrice kills me. 'Often late to bed makes a girl unfit to wed.'" I rolled my eyes. "See you tomorrow."

She waved a manicured hand. "See you tomorrow, cupcake."

I grinned as the doorbell chimed above my head. *Cupcake? What next, Charlie Cooper?*

* * * * *

I sat in the window seat, staring out at the moon again. It was so bright tonight — like a nice, glowing gumdrop that I could just pluck from the sky and suck on.

I smiled and pulled out my notebook.

May 30, 1943

Dear Mama,

I tapped my pen on the nearly empty page.

Dear Mama, I ...

I pulled my blue-striped pajamas closer and looked out the window. A nice night for a walk.

The water felt so good on my bare toes. I closed my eyes and smiled, remembering how nice it felt to be covered in it yesterday, freezing as it was.

The wind danced through my hair. *Allie*, it whispered, *Allie ...*

"The moon is distant from the sea," someone whispered in my ear. I screamed and whipped around: Sam Carroll. He seemed unfazed by the interruption and continued to recite, "And yet with amber hands she leads him, docile as a boy, along appointed sands."

My chest was still pounding. "What are you doing here?"

He stuck his hands in his pockets and smiled. His hair was mussed again. "That was Dickinson."

I glared at him. "I know that was Dickinson." What did he think I was, stupid?

"Oh, and so you've read Dickinson?" He cocked an eyebrow.

"Yes, I know Dickinson, and yes, I've read that poem. It was very pretty." I leveled my eyes. "How do *you* know it?"

"I've read Dickinson." Sam looked me up and down and smirked a little. "Nice pajamas."

I crossed my arms, looking out at the ocean. "Why are you here?"

"Why are *you* here?"

"I couldn't sleep."

"Neither could I."

I stomped my foot. "Oh, why are you so impossible?"

"*I'm* impossible?" He paused for a second. "I beg your pardon, miss. Perhaps you're used to men throwing themselves at your feet."

That was it. That was *it*! "You are following me."

Sam spread out his hands. "Guilty as charged."

My eyes widened. "What are—"

Sam raised his eyes to the sky. "I'm just joking. Honestly, Allie. I may have come to Maine and everything, but do you really think I knew I was going to find you out here in the middle of the night?"

I gulped. "So what are you doing here?"

"I told you: I couldn't sleep."

Why is he so annoying? I heaved a breath. "What are you doing on this beach?"

"I'm staying with my aunt Rachel, as you know." He pointed to a big yellow house on the hill. "She lives right—"

"I know where she lives!" I snapped. *Whoa. Calm down, Allie.* I took a deep breath and wiggled my toes in the sand. "Sorry. So why are you being so nice?"

Sam wrinkled his forehead. "Was I ever not nice?"

"No one's truly nice." I glanced up at him. "Besides, you tried to drown me yesterday."

"If I recall correctly, the favor was returned."

Was he smiling? I felt a shell under my bare foot and reached down to pick it up, turning it over so all the sand ran out. "So …"

I looked up. Sam was staring at me. I squirmed. "What?"

"Nothing." Sam dropped his gaze and kicked at the sand. "I'm just trying to figure out who you are."

"I thought you—"

Sam chuckled. "I don't actually mean who you are. I mean who you are as a person. It's been awhile since I last saw you. Maybe you've changed." He squinted at me, as if trying to memorize my features in the dim moonlight. "Are you the dull, lifeless person who sulks around parties, or the lively sprite who tumbles around in the ocean?"

I laughed and splashed water on his clean trousers. He ducked and kicked back. I squealed and ran down the ocean-front, spraying water everywhere, not caring if Beatrice saw or heard.

* * * * *

The stars were so bright and clear. And so distant.

"How many stars do you think there are?" Sam whispered.

"Don't know." I sighed and shifted a little, the cold, hard rock firm underneath me. I craned my neck so I could see Sam lying on a rock only a few feet from me, staring up at the same sky. "Billions, I guess." I sat up, overcome with an urge to impress him. I bit the corner of my mouth and pointed at the constellation Taurus. "See that star?"

"What star?" Sam raised himself a little.

"That one, the third brightest." I settled back on the rock and smiled. "It's called Alcyone."

"Really?" Sam squinted up at it, interested. "It's beautiful."

"I know," I whispered. "When it rises, it means the cold autumn is coming."

"Oh."

We sat in silence for a long while, staring up at the heavens above us. My heart squeezed for a moment, thinking about Mama and how much she enjoyed stargazing.

"So tell me about this Beatrice Lovell." Sam propped up his elbow. "Is she your mom now?"

"No." My voice was cold and flat. I cringed and looked away.

"But I though she said—"

"Beatrice lives in a state of delusion." I stared up at my namesake star. "She thinks we're this idyllic little mother and daughter family and that everything is perfect and she chose me because she knows I'm ... as wonderful as she is or something." I scowled at the sky. The stars didn't seem so friendly anymore. Now they were just teasing me—playing with my emotions.

"So ... she adopted you?"

"I came here only because I had to."

Sam stared at me for a second. "It can't be that bad. She seems nice, I mean."

"She's okay." I sighed. "It's just ... she wants to be my mom. She's always trying to figure out how I feel and trying to get into my head. And constantly trying to get me to open up to her." My voice hardened. "She's not my mom."

"Oh."

I turned to look at Sam again. He was studying the stars with a sort of fierce frown on his face, so different from the dopey little Sam Carroll I used to know, and yet so much the same.

"So what about your family, Sam? Why are you here in Maine?"

He exhaled slowly. "Robert died."

I sat up straight. "Your *brother*?" Sweet Robby with the blue eyes and dimples? "How?"

"Killed in action." Sam caught my dismayed face and gave me a wan smile. "Mother and Father don't support the war, so he ran off last summer to enlist. He was fifteen."

I felt sick to my stomach. "Sam, I had no idea … I …"

Sam shook his head and gave me that thin little smile again. "Don't. I'm kind of sick of hearing it."

I watched him for a few seconds more, waiting to see if he'd say anything else. "Oh." I eased myself back onto the rock. The wind changed, sending a warm breeze of sea salt in our direction. I licked my lips and stayed silent.

"Did you really know that poem I recited earlier?" Sam asked.

"Every word." I traced letters on the rock with my finger. " 'The Moon is Distant from the Sea.' I've always liked it." I shot him a smile. "But you must have found that out somehow."

Sam held up a hand. "Lucky guess. I swear."

I raised an eyebrow. "You know, you don't strike me as the kind who memorizes poetry."

"And you don't strike me as the kind who writes it."

I shot up again. "How did you—"

"Relax." Sam spread out his hands. "I saw it on the page of that journal you were scribbling in yesterday. Don't look at me like that: I promise I didn't read it. I just saw the first line."

Giving him my darkest look, I growled, "You'd better not tell Beatrice. No one knows about what's in that notebook. Not even Charlie. I'd kill you if—"

"Charlie?" Sam was looking at me funny.

"A girlfriend. Charlie Cooper. She lives right over—" I began to point.

"I know where the Coopers live," Sam snapped in a girly voice.

I paused for a minute, then allowed myself to smile. *Touché.* "Sorry."

"So, does this … Charlie … write poetry too?"

I snorted. "Hardly."

"So who inspired you?"

I took a deep breath. "Mama." I looked at him and tried to look happy. He was watching me intently, as if I were an insect or something. I squirmed and focused on the rock. "It was her dream for me to become a famous poet. Our dream." I swallowed. "I'm going to do it one day."

My heart crumbled a little around the edges; I'd put all thoughts about my life with her out of my mind a long time ago.

"You know, I can remember what she was like before the sickness," Sam said, rubbing his hands together. "I never did see her much, but the few times I did she was really sweet. She treated me like I was an adult, not a little kid." He turned and looked at me. "I think you're a lot like her."

"Really?" I smiled. "How so?"

Sam shrugged. "Your mother lived out her fantasies. And I think you live out yours too."

I barked out a laugh. "You think it's my fantasy to live here in Maine?"

He shook his head. "No. It's to write."

"Yeah. I guess you're right." I pressed my lips together.

Sam took a deep breath and let it out. "I'm sorry, Allie. I know it must have hurt."

I twisted the end of my pajama top around my finger and then let it go. "Not at first. But as she got worse ... the things people said ... That's what hurt. They called her crazy. It got to the point where I couldn't even go into town anymore." My eyelids slid shut, blocking out the tears. I cleared my throat and tried again.

I bit the side of my mouth and tried to swallow the lump in my throat. What was this? I never cried anymore. I was like these ocean-side rocks now. *Firm, steady.* "I didn't understand how people could be so cruel. So judgmental." I shrugged and trailed to a stop, not trusting myself to talk.

Sam was silent. Listening. And I realized he was the only one who might truly understand what I'd gone through.

I cleared my throat. "We never went out anymore. You know that." I peeked at him between closed lids. "After that I took care of her; took care of the house. I made the meals and cleaned and looked after the cat. Right on up until she died. Sometimes ..." I opened my eyes again, but this time the stars were blurry. Unrecognizable. "I would have kept on doing it, Sam. I would have kept on cleaning forever if it had kept her alive. Honest."

I turned and looked at him. He was watching me. Sam smiled a little and nodded. "I know."

An awkward silence fell over us. I shook off my tears and settled back on the rock. "Um, can you see the Big Dipper?"

Sam pointed at the sky. "Up there. It's the one that kinda looks like a crooked pencil."

"It does not!"

"Does too!" he protested. "See it, there? Hmm? A crooked pencil, I'm telling you!"

I huffed and jumped up. "I'm leaving. You're a bore, Sam Carroll." I could hear him laughing as I walked back up the beach alone.

"Allie!"

I turned and waited, a teasing grin ready.

Sam smiled. "You haven't changed."

My stomach tickled. "Thank you." I paused. "I'm glad."

Chapter 9

I'm nobody! Who are you?
Are you nobody, too?
Then there's a pair of us — don't tell!
They'd banish us, you know.

—Emily Dickinson

I opened the back door and crept through the kitchen. A light was on in the library. Not good.

I put one foot on the staircase, and was met with a loud creak. I cringed. *Please, no, please …*

"Allie?"

I sighed and trudged into the library, where Beatrice was sitting in her reading chair, a book discarded in her lap. She took off her glasses and looked up at me.

"Alcyone Lovell," she said, crossing her arms. "Would you please read me the time on that clock?"

I glanced at it. "Two thirty."

"AM?"

I refused to answer, looking down at my bare toes on the Oriental rug.

Beatrice heaved a heavy breath. "Allie, where have you been?"

I glanced up. There was genuine concern on her face, stinging my conscience. "You wouldn't care," I muttered, kicking the floor.

That caught her attention. "What do you mean? Allie, I've been sitting here for over an hour ..."

"Of course you've been sitting here." I crossed my arms. "You're always sitting there ... So patient. So perfect. Just waiting for me and my stupid mistakes to mess up your life again."

Beatrice's face flushed. "Now listen here, Alcyone," she said, her voice quiet but firm. "This is *my* house and in it we abide by *my* rules. And I will not have you—"

"Your house?" My voice broke and I slid into the armchair across from her. "Of course it's *your house*. It's always been *your house*. This has never been *my house*." A tear slipped down my cheek. I brushed at it and looked down.

All the anger and frustrations of the past four years still felt bottled up inside me. It seemed like I was always hurting— always lashing out. But the issues never really felt settled.

"Alcyone." Beatrice sounded pained. I knew she was probably tired and didn't feel like having this conversation again right now, but she pressed on. "Allie, I've always wanted this to be our house. I've always wanted us to be a family." She reached out and placed her slightly wrinkled hand over mine, squeezing it.

I knew she meant it. She meant every word of it. She was the perfect mother and I was the ungrateful adopted child. It was only by her charity that I had a roof over my head, much less a place I was supposed to call "home."

My eyes stung. "Sorry," I muttered. "I'm just ... I'm just sorry." I ducked my head and walked out of the room. *A family. Sure.*

"Allie?" Beatrice called.

"Good night."

I ran up the stairs and shut the door of my room, collapsing on the bed. *A fine family this is.*

I heard footsteps in the hallway and someone knocking on the door. "Allie?" Beatrice, of course. "Allie, can we just get this out? Just talk about it?"

I answered her with silence.

"Allie?"

I muffled my sobs into my pillow and waited until I heard the footsteps retreating. Then I rolled around and fell asleep.

* * * * *

Charlie looped her arm and mine and giggled like a true Southern belle. "So," she drawled, looking around at the rationed items on the grocery shelf. *Tuna fish? No. Green beans? No.* "If you don't want Russell Wilkinson, honey, can I please have him?"

I widened my eyes and looked around. We were in a *grocery store.* People were probably *listening,* for heaven's sake. "Charlie," I hissed, "you make him sound as if he were an item on our list!"

Charlie pursed her scarlet lips. "Allie, sweetie, I'm serious."

She probably was. I took a deep breath and picked up a loaf of bread. "Charlie," I said, making sure to keep my voice low, "what would you possibly want with Russell? I thought you were waiting for some tall, dark, European stranger or something."

Charlie rolled her eyes. "The Europeans turned out to be jerks. Look what they got us into." She smiled and squeezed my arm. "No, honey, rich is the way to go." She wiggled her pencil-thin eyebrows. "And Russell certainly has that down to a point."

I couldn't help laughing as I picked up a box of cereal and dropped it into my basket. We continued down the aisle, grinning widely at the people around us. "Charlie," I said out of the side of my mouth. "He's five foot six and carries around a pet poodle."

Charlie examined a box and smiled coyly. "I've always considered myself a dog lover."

"More like a gold lover," I muttered.

"Cash, dear! Cold hard cash! Besides, Russell's not bad looking. You make him sound absolutely dreadful."

I raised my eyebrows and dragged Charlie toward the checkout. The boy behind the counter helped us load our groceries and rang them up. I exhaled obnoxiously at Charlie. "I suppose if you're into the gangly, feminized type ..."

"Allie!"

"What?" I widened my eyes innocently. Then I saw Charlie's face. She was serious. I composed my features and pulled out my ration stamps, handing them to the grocer. "Fine. You can have Russell, if you really want him. I'll try to break the news to him tomorrow." *There's nothing I'd enjoy more.*

"Thank you, darling! I owe you." Charlie reached over and squeezed me, her perfume overwhelming my nose for a brief second. But I smiled and squeezed her back.

A bell dinged at the front of the shop and Debra Wilkinson

sashayed in. When she spotted us, her eyes lit up. I cringed and tried to avert my face, but Charlie grabbed my arm. I shot her a look before turning to smile at Debra. "Here's your chance," I whispered out of the side of my mouth. "Impress Russell's mother."

"Allie and Charlotte!" Debra cooed as she rushed up to us, holding out her arms. "What a lovely surprise!"

"Mrs. Wilkinson," I oozed back.

"Allie, darling, did Beatrice tell you about a little party I'm hosting next week? It's a sort of benefit — you know, for the war effort. I *do* hope you can come." She simpered at Charlie as an afterthought. "Both of you."

"I'm sorry, Mrs. Wilkinson, but I — " *Ouch.* Charlie had dug her clawlike fingernails into my arm. I fought back a wince.

"We'd love to," Charlie purred, flashing Mrs. Wilkinson one of her hundred-watt smiles.

I tried to discreetly shake my head at her, but she refused to look my way. I grinned, trying to mask my pain. "I'll pass the message on to Beatrice."

"Oh, thank you, Allie! You're an angel!" Mrs. Wilkinson beamed at me. I thought I saw her raise an eyebrow coolly to Charlie before passing on.

As soon as she was out of sight, I dropped the smile and ripped Charlie's hand off my arm. "What were you thinking? Do you want me to die of mental insanity at that party?"

Charlie's eyes shot to the ceiling. "Allie, it can't be that bad. Besides, where else would I wear my blue gingham and ensure that Russell sees me?"

The thought of trying to impress Russell made me gag.

I grabbed my bags from the clerk and turned to go. "Really, Charlie, don't you think you're being a little —"

"Who's Russell?" a voice asked.

I yelped and whipped around. Sam Carroll was standing behind me with that silly smirk, his hands in his pockets. I put a hand over my mouth. "You scared me."

"So I see." Sam gave me a wry look. "Seems to be a habit of mine."

"Russell is a friend," Charlie said. "A good friend. And you are?"

Sam swept into a bow right in the middle of the grocery store. "Sam Carroll, your ladyship."

Charlie giggled as he kissed her hand. "Delighted."

This was sort of sick. Sam and Charlie?

"Sam, this is Charlotte Cooper," I muttered.

"May I call you Charlie, Miss Cooper?" Sam asked, the perfect gentleman.

"I shall be quite mad if you don't."

Whatever happened to Russell? The girl was positively fickle!

I flung one of the brown paper bags at Charlie before slinging the other on my hip, suddenly feeling like an ugly duckling stuck outside the pond. I glared at Sam and looped my arm through Charlie's. "We were just leaving, actually. Good-bye, Sam."

Sam raised an eyebrow, amused. "Bye."

I tried to hold my head up as we walked out of the door. Or rather, I walked, while Charlie more or less strutted. Did she have to wear such high heels? To the *grocery store*?

"Who was that?" Charlie whispered, looking over her shoulder.

"An old friend."

Charlie smiled. "I'd like to get to know him."

I'm sure you would. I avoided her eye as I loaded the groceries into the car.

"What?" Charlie stared at me, looking confused.

Did I say that out loud? I bit my lip, my brain scrambling for a way to explain my ugly remark.

Charlie turned slowly and placed a hand on her hip. She watched me, curious. "Is there something going on between you and him?"

"What?" I tried to laugh, slamming the car door shut. "I don't know what you're talking about."

"Yeah, clearly." A smile played around in the corner of Charlie's mouth. "I'm not being serious, if that makes you feel better. I could care less about Sam Carroll."

The way she said his name bothered me. It sounded sneaky, like she was waiting to get my reaction.

I brushed my hair over my shoulder and shrugged. "Like I said, I don't know what you're talking about."

"Right." Charlie laughed and hopped in the passenger seat. "Sure."

* * * * *

Bing Crosby was playing as I walked in the front door. I dropped my keys on the table and looked around, confused. "Beatrice?" I called as I pulled off my sweater.

Beatrice never listened to Bing or Fred or Louis. The only music she ever played in *her house* were records from the turn of the century, when she was some kind of debutante in Maine.

"Allie, is that you?"

I walked toward the parlor. "Yeah, I just got back from——"
I walked into the room and froze. In the loveseat was the back
of a young woman.

Beatrice smiled. "Look who just walked in."

The woman turned her head and grinned, showing perfect
white teeth behind hot pink lipstick. "How *are* you, darling?"

I screamed and dropped the groceries. "Irene!"

She laughed and held out her arms, which I ran into. I closed
my eyes and breathed in. She smelled just the same — perfume
mixed with cherry soda. Sometimes I thought Irene was the
only good thing that came with my moving in with Beatrice.
She pulled back and looked me over. "*Gosh*, honey, I've *missed*
you! It's been what? Three months?" She squeezed my shoulder.
"It's so good to be home!"

I let her hug me. Even hugged her back, a little bit. "How
was Florida?"

She widened her eyes and laughed. "Hot. I don't know *how*
Daniel stands that heat every day. One *hour* in the military
would kill me."

I smiled. "Well, a training camp isn't nearly as bad as the
actual fighting front."

An awkward silence filled the room. Irene looked pained.
Beatrice coughed and shook her head at me. "I'm sure Daniel
will handle it well," she said, but the cheer in her voice didn't
show up in her eyes. "I've always said that a strong will can stand
the harshest drill."

"Yes, well, I suppose you're right. God is with him, I know.
Protecting him and getting him ready to come back to me

soon." Irene winked and sat back down on the loveseat, scooting over for me to sit beside her. "*So*, darling, Mom was just bragging on you. She said you won a writing award with a check for *fifty dollars*. Out of *everyone* in the *school*!"

I blushed and ducked my head.

Irene wiggled her eyebrows. "I always *knew* our girl had it in her. She'll grow up to be *famous* yet!"

I fidgeted in my seat and tried to look happy. She didn't mean to upset me, after all. Irene squeezed my arm with her long pink nails as she looked around the parlor. "*Gosh*, Mom, you really need to redecorate. It's been like this since I was a girl!" She laughed. "This place looks *centuries* old!"

Beatrice chuckled and folded her hands in her lap. "I always have been one for tradition. You may have gotten me to play that confounded record, Irene, but you will not convince me to redecorate my home. Not in a million years."

My home. Did she realize how often she said that? I recrossed my legs.

"Allie, I heard there was a certain *something* going on between you and a young fellow here," Irene said with false brightness. She looked at Beatrice and winked.

I blushed. *How did she ...*

"A young man by the name of Russell, perhaps?" Irene's eyebrows danced.

Oh. I shook my head. "No, no, there's ... really nothing going on between us."

"Oh, pish-posh." Beatrice beamed at Irene. "Russell's crazy about Allie."

Much to my discomfort. I pretended to enjoy the conversation and took the time to study Irene. Her bright red hair was fading into a burnt auburn, her flawless skin was wrinkling just a little around the eyes and mouth. Even her eyes had clouded over a little.

Is time away from your husband that difficult, or did I just not notice her aging before? I frowned. *She can still hardly be much older than thirty.*

"Well," Beatrice said, pushing away from the table. "I'd better go get supper on. You two keep on talking." She gazed at us a moment more before walking out, humming contentedly to herself.

Irene watched her leave and smiled, her eyes crinkling. "I'm so glad she's happy," she said. "You're taking such good care of her, Allie. I wouldn't trust her with anyone else." Irene laughed and nudged me. "She's a special woman. She deserves to be taken care of, you know?" She lowered her voice. "She's blessed to have a daughter like you." As she stroked my hand, her eyes clouded over.

I nodded and forced the corners of my mouth up, but I felt hollow and my stomach ached. Didn't Irene know that ... that *glow* in Beatrice's eyes was all for her? Her *true* daughter. Once Irene left, all the sunshine would go with her.

Beatrice never looks at me that way. Every time she glanced in my direction, I sensed nothing but tiredness and concealed frustration. I was something she dutifully cared for, not loved. I cleared my throat and looked away.

Irene looked at the empty doorway a moment more before giggling and hopping off the loveseat. "I'm going to go help

120

Mom out with supper. You relax." She smiled and skipped out of the room like a six-year-old.

I sighed and pulled my feet up onto the armchair.

"I looooove you," someone crooned from the gramophone.

I glared at it. "Oh, shut up."

Chapter 10

Delight is as the flight —
Or in the Ratio of it,
As the Schools would say —
The Rainbow's way.

—Emily Dickinson

Irene squeezed my elbow and laughed. "Oh, I haven't been to a picture show in *years*, girls! Daniel never can go."

Charlie's eyes twinkled. "This one has Clark Gable in it. He's the dreamiest star *ever*. Or so Allie thinks." She wiggled her eyebrows.

I blushed and walked up to the window. "Three for *Gone with the Wind*." I looked over my shoulder at Irene. "It came out a few years ago, but it's still good."

When the lady behind the desk gave us our tickets, Irene giggled like a girl. "Oh, it's so *exciting!*" She pushed up her sunglasses and squeezed Charlie's arm.

Charlie gave me a quizzical look, and I could tell she was holding back a laugh.

"So, Allie," Irene said, smiling at me. "I ran into quite the interesting young man at the post office the other day. He told me you were friends when you were younger."

I clutched my ticket, creasing it down the middle. "Sam?"

"Yeah." Irene brightened. "I invited him to the movies with us today."

"You did *what*?"

"Ladies," someone said behind us. I turned around slowly. It was only Russell. My heart stopped racing before I'd even realized it had started.

"You silly boy!" Charlie gushed, grabbing his arm. "What brings *you* here?"

Irene looked between the two of them and crossed her arms knowingly.

"Lovely day for a picture show. Don't you think so, Allie?" He smiled at me and held up his ticket.

"Sure, Russell."

"Good afternoon, everyone."

I turned again, this time to see Sam Carroll tip his hat at us. "One for the Clark Gable show," he said to the girl behind the counter.

"Oh, it's you again!" Charlie beamed at him and then turned back to Russell, reaching up to play with a tendril in her golden bob.

"Good afternoon," Irene said, nodding. Sam tipped his hat in response.

"Who is this?" Russell frowned at him.

"Oh, it's just Sam." I rolled my eyes. "Irene invited him to come with us."

Russell went back to looking disapprovingly at Sam. "How do you know Allie?"

Sam winked at me. "We go way back." He smiled as he took his ticket from the blushing girl behind the counter.

Charlie squeezed Russell's arm, not that he seemed to notice. "Well, this is just lovely. It's like a double date! With Irene, of course."

"Of course." Irene grabbed her purse and began to walk into the theater. "I'll see you inside, Allie." She looked at me with the same knowing look she'd given Charlie.

What? I turned to face Sam, who was grinning.

"We're right behind you!" Charlie pulled Russell, who continued to frown back at Sam and me, into the theater. "Terrible weather, isn't it, darling?" She shivered, glancing up at the stubbornly blue sky. Russell hesitated before wrapping his arm around her.

I snuck a look at Sam. He held out his elbow to me. "Shall we?"

I stormed into the theater, leaving him to follow me in. Knowing him, he probably was amused by it.

* * * * *

Clark Gable was just too handsome. I stuffed popcorn into my mouth and sighed. *Really, that woman just doesn't deserve him.*

"I don't get it," Sam whispered.

I glared at him. Didn't he ever hear you were supposed to be *quiet* during the picture show?

"Why do women love him so much? He's not that great looking." Sam reached over for a handful of popcorn.

I ripped the popcorn away from him. "Are you serious? *Clark Gable?*"

Sam smirked. "Yeah."

I looked back at the screen. *What does he know?*

Sam reached over and brushed a piece of popcorn off my sleeve. "What's wrong?"

Charlie, who was sitting behind us and obviously listening, leaned forward and grinned. "You don't know what you've started. Allie's had a crush on Gable since she was fifteen."

Sam's eyebrows shot up. "Really? I guess I wouldn't know, considering she and I never went to movie theaters in Tennessee."

I squirmed, keeping my eyes glued on the screen.

"Mmm-hmm." Charlie propped her elbows up on our seats, her mouth close to my ears.

Sam looked like he was holding back a laugh. I glared at Charlie and stuffed more popcorn into my mouth.

"Hey, I've got an idea," Charlie whispered in our ears.

I started to frown. "Now, that's never a good thing—"

"Hush!" Charlie lowered her voice. "There's a fair in town. I say we ditch the picture show and go have some fun." She raised one side of her mouth. "What do you say?"

"I'm up for it." Sam started to stand. I grabbed his shirt and pulled him back down.

"What about Irene?" I hissed.

Charlie widened her eyes innocently. "What about her?"

"We can't just leave her."

Charlie shrugged and leaned over to Irene before I could stop her. "Hey, Irene, honey, is it okay if we go over to the fair? It's getting a bit stuffy in here." She fanned herself and batted her eyelashes.

Irene laughed and swatted us with her purse. "Go on, you silly kids. I'll cover for you." She saw me and grinned. "What? I was young once too." She lowered her voice so only I could hear her. "And it's a great night for love."

My mouth dropped open. "No, no, it's not ..."

She snuck a quick look at Sam and whispered, "Trust me, just go and have fun," then settled back into her seat.

Beside me, I think Sam was smiling. *Did he ...?* My face grew scarlet as I climbed out of our row.

Gosh, why did I have to be adopted by such an embarrassing family?

✳ ✳ ✳ ✳ ✳

The fairground was alive with glowing lights, with the sweet smells of popcorn and cotton candy wafting through the air.

"I honestly thought you were going to get sick on that last ride, Allie," Sam said into my ear, his eyes twinkling.

I leveled my eyes at him. "I'm sure you would have enjoyed that."

Sam shrugged his shoulders and grabbed a piece of popcorn. "Hey, I'm not saying I would have liked it to happen. But if it did, I would have wanted to see it."

Charlie laughed and shoved him. "Oh, you are too much! Isn't he too much, Allie?"

"You have no idea," I muttered.

Sam looked up. "What's that?"

"Nothing." I looked away and instead focused on the twirling lights of the merry-go-round.

"And that's when I discovered that botany isn't so different from biophysics after all," Russell droned on beside me, idly chewing on a piece of popcorn. "It all depends on the chemical makeup of—"

"Oh, a Ferris wheel!" Charlie brightened, grabbing my arm. She tugged my elbow and batted her eyelashes. "Oh, let's go on it, Allie. Come on!" She giggled and linked her arm through Russell's. "Have you ever been on a Ferris wheel, Russell? It's so much fun!"

Sam and I followed and climbed into the seat above them. The ride conductor shouted and pulled back the lever, setting the wheel in motion.

The ride started slowly. I took a deep breath, determined not to show my fear. It was just so ... high. I clutched the side of the seat and looked over the edge, and my stomach churned in response. I sat back and closed my eyes.

Sam was laughing. "Haven't you ever ridden a Ferris wheel before?"

"Once." I opened one eye. "I threw up." I promptly closed the eye, my face reddening.

"Well then, this will be interesting," Sam chuckled. I reached out and slapped his arm. "No need for violence. Just sayin' that if it happens ..."

Breathe in. Breathe out. This will all be over soon.

The ride jolted to a stop. My eyes jerked open. We were almost at the top of the Ferris wheel, looking down at the brightly lit park.

Panicked, I clutched Sam's jacket. "What happened?"

A short, bald man walked over to the side of the ride. "Just hold on!" he shouted. "We're having a few problems, but we're sure it will be fixed in no time at all!"

127

Sam smiled and nodded at him. He turned to me with a devilish smirk on his face. "Looks like you'll be getting over your fear tonight."

I grimaced, my stomach feeling woozy.

* * * * *

"How are you all doing up there?"

Sam waved to the man below. *If he wasn't the only thing keeping me somewhat calm, I would throw him over the side.*

I groaned and pulled my thin sweater tight. "We've been up here for two hours."

I looked down at the park beneath us. In time, my wooziness had settled to a slight flutter at the sight of all the lights and little people below, though I was far from happy to be perched in the air. At least everyone had stopped staring at the stuck Ferris wheel and were now continuing on their way out of the park.

Sam smiled. "It's a beautiful evening."

I stared at him, incredulous. "The park is closing in ten minutes. This evening won't be beautiful for long."

"Allie?"

I looked down to see Russell glancing up at me with owl eyes. On his shoulder, Charlie had dozed off. "What, Russell?"

"I have to go to the bathroom," Russell whispered, his face red.

Sam shrugged. "Sorry." He whispered to me, "What does he think you can do about it?"

Russell grimaced and tried to go back to sleep.

I in turn sighed and leaned on the side of the seat.

Sam fiddled with his ride tickets. "I wish there was some kind of poem I could recite about this."

"There is no poem about this." I turned and settled my gaze on him. "How many poets have gotten stuck on a Ferris wheel two hours after curfew? Not even Irene can get me out of this one."

Sam grinned. "Maybe I'll write one instead." His brow knotted as if he was deep in thought. "I shall call it 'Ode to a Luminous Wheel.'" He glanced sideways at me and batted his eyelashes. "I'll dedicate it to you."

A smile tugged at my lips. "I doubt you could write poetry." Before the smile could betray me, I turned away, clutching the side of the seat while looking out over the park.

"You'd be surprised."

I strummed the hard steel seats, trying to keep my mouth straight.

"Do you remember your fourteenth birthday?" Sam asked suddenly.

My head shot around. He was staring at me, an unreadable expression on his face. I lowered my eyes.

Sam folded and refolded a ticket. "I gave you a set of chalks." He looked seriously in my eyes. "Did you really hate them as much as you made it seem?"

My stomach lurched. "No," I said softly.

"Oh." Sam ran a hand through his hair and then looked away. "Just wondering."

"And, um ..." My voice choked. "And what I said at the funeral wasn't true, either. About Mama's death being your fault and all." I looked down at my lap.

"Oh, good. I felt really bad. For, you know, keeping you from being there and everything."

"No, I'm glad I wasn't there." The words took me by surprise. "I wouldn't have wanted to see Mama fall and feel like … Like it was my fault."

"Yeah?" I studied the floor, but I felt his gaze. My stomach fluttered.

"Yeah."

* * * * *

"Allie?" Beatrice glanced at me out of the corner of her eye.

"Hmm?" I rested my head against the car window and closed my eyes. Lights buzzed past us as we drove through the busiest part of town. Beatrice paused. I peeked open an eye and saw her gripping the steering wheel, her knuckles white.

"Allie …" We turned into our driveway and stopped at the top of the hill. I leaned over to climb out, but Beatrice grabbed my arm. "Allie, wait."

I jerked back into the seat. "What?"

Beatrice sighed. I couldn't see her face in the dark car. *Has she decided to punish me after all? I'm still surprised she let Irene take the blame and let me off the hook that easily.*

I squirmed. The silence was awkward.

"Is it something I did?" Beatrice finally asked.

"What are you talking about?"

Beatrice took a deep breath. "Ever since you came here you've been … bent-up and moody and … I don't know. It feels like you're holding everything inside, deep down … somewhere. It can't be good for you, Allie. But I can't figure out what I've done or what I can do to make you happy. You know how I pray for you. That God would lead you to show me what's wrong."

I gulped. *I don't need your prayers.* "There's nothing wrong." I adjusted my yellow cotton skirt and tried to open the car door.

"Allie." She reached out to grab my arm, her voice softly pleading. "I've never tried to do anything to hurt you. All I've wanted to do is be a good mother to you — to love you."

My head whipped around. "I have a mother and I have a home and neither one is in Maine."

Her face crumpled. She dropped her hand and turned to the steering wheel, tears filling her eyes.

My stomach churned for the second time that night. I opened my mouth and shut it. *I shouldn't have ...* "Sorry," I whispered.

I jumped out of the car and slammed the door, running to the house and up the stairs.

I locked my bedroom door and collapsed on the window seat. *I'm so stupid. Why can't I do anything right?*

I banged my fist against the wall and covered my face. "Why does this have to be so hard?" I whispered.

I glanced out the window. Beatrice was leaning on the side of the car, burying her face in her arm.

My heart squeezed with guilt. I closed my eyes. *Mama. I want Mama.*

She'd said that Christians would do their best to make you feel wanted. To make religion sound so good and inviting. But I couldn't crack. I had to stand firm.

I could hear her voice in my head: "All people want to do is hurt you. All you can trust is where you come from and who you are."

I glanced out the window and saw Beatrice wiping her cheeks, turning to come inside.

I pulled the curtains shut and wrapped my arms around my knees. My eyes welled up. "I don't care," I whispered into the darkness. "I don't care."

Chapter 11

I cannot dance upon my Toes—
No Man instructed me—
But oftentimes, among my mind,
A Glee possesseth me.

—Emily Dickinson

I sat at my vanity and stuck my tongue out at the mirror. *I look like a madman.*

I pulled my tongue back in and tried to form an honest impression of myself. A pale, fluttery creature stared back at me, clad in airy green chiffon with deep brown waves and cherry lips. She was far too fine to be Allie Everly.

I sighed and stood, grabbing a pair of pumps from the closet. I glanced in the mirror one last time and adjusted my sash. A small smile threatened to escape my mouth.

"Allie!" Beatrice called. "The party started ten minutes ago!"

I pulled on the shoes and shut the bedroom door behind me. Beatrice looked up from across the hall and halted, her chin dropping. She put a hand up to her mouth leaned against the stairwell. "Oh, Allie," she whispered, "you look lovely."

I let the smile escape. "Thank you." I pranced down the stairs. "I suppose we should get going."

"Russell will like that dress," Beatrice commented as she opened the car door. "A pretty girl makes a man's thoughts whirl," she teased in a sing-song voice.

"I highly doubt he'll notice it." The thought lifted my spirits higher. "He's been a bit preoccupied with Charlie as of late."

Beatrice raised an eyebrow, clearly interested. "Really?" She seemed to ponder this in silence for a while. "That's a good match for Charlie," she decided.

"Mmm-hmm." I leaned my cheek on the car window and watched the houses whizz by, bathed in the warm glow of the setting sun.

"You know, you really do look stunning, Allie," Beatrice said, looking over at me. "I truly am proud of you."

I lowered my eyes. *She's probably just saying that so I won't sulk and embarrass her.* Nevertheless, I felt a wave of pride surge inside me — one I intended to keep private. "Thanks," I muttered.

Beatrice looked at me intently for a few moments before sighing loudly. She parked the car in front of the Wilkinson's house and climbed out, while I sat by myself just long enough to make her frustrated before I followed her into the house.

A Billie Holiday song greeted us as we entered, followed by a smiling Debra Wilkinson. "Beatrice and Allie!" She rushed over and enveloped us into her perfumed arms. "I'm so glad you're here!" She looked around with a creased brow. "And where is Irene?"

Beatrice gracefully extracted herself from Mrs. Wilkinson's arms. "She returned to Florida for the rest of the summer, until Daniel finishes training. I believe she'll be home again in October."

"Isn't that nice?" Mrs. Wilkinson glanced at me and pinched my arm. "The young people are gathered on the terrace, Allie dear." She winked and shooed me outside.

Once the adults were out of sight, I shivered. The sight of Mrs. Wilkinson's overly made-up face so close to mine was burned into my permanent memory.

Charlie's laughter drifted over the terrace. I caught sight of her blonde curls through the sea of people and made my way toward her.

Russell and Sam, as well as about a dozen other boys from school, were standing nearby, engrossed in whatever she was saying. If she wasn't my friend, I'd be almost jealous.

Charlie caught sight of me and waved, her entire face coming alive. "Allie! Oh, Allie, how are you?" She pulled me close and hugged me, the scent of her perfume much sweeter than Debra Wilkinson's.

I smiled at all the young men briefly before grabbing Charlie's arm and pulling her aside. She giggled and squeezed my elbow, biting her lip. "Say, Allie, do I look okay? I caught Russell staring at me a few minutes ago."

I snorted. "Charlie, every young man over there was gawking at you just now. How do you think you look?"

Charlie blushed and smoothed her blue gingham dress. She glanced me up and down and looked almost as shocked as Miss Beatrice. "You look nice."

"Thank you." I grabbed her elbow and turned back to the young men. They straightened, smiling at us. "What was Charlie telling you all?" I asked.

"She was telling us about a puppy she found on the side of the road last week," Russell answered, pulling at his necktie. He smiled at Charlie, looking more dopey than usual. "It was wonderful."

Charlie beamed and looked down.

A new record started up, a jazzy waltz coming from the gramophone. Russell glanced at Charlie. "Would you like to dance?"

She shrugged, though her eyes were shining brilliantly. "I don't see why not."

I watched him lead her into the living room, until they disappeared behind a crowd of dancing couples. I crinkled my nose. *Isn't that cute?* I turned to see all the young men staring at one boy from school, who watched me nervously.

"Say, Allie," he croaked, "you wanna dance?"

I raised an eyebrow. "Not with you, Teddy Buchanan." Almost as second nature, I glanced the rest of the boys over, daring them with my haughtiness. One by one, they each dropped their eyes. Only Sam continued to watch me, an unreadable look on his face.

Without another word, I spun on my heel and marched back inside the house, not sure whether or not to be ashamed of myself. I wasn't sweet—that much was true. But I didn't like to think of myself as a total brat. At least not in front of Sam.

I stood in a doorway, watching the dancing couples swing by. Charlie looked blissfully happy, laughing at everything Russell had to say. And Russell, for his part, looked like the proudest man in the room.

The record died down, and the old hit "Cheek to Cheek" started. I swished my green skirts around me and stood on my tiptoes, gently swaying with the music. It was such a happy song.

I bent my head and twirled around, imagining I was dancing with a partner. A hand pressed against my back as someone grabbed my waist and began to lead me. I looked up to see Sam smiling down at me.

"Hi," he said.

"Hi." I looked away, feeling my entire body turn red, but let him escort me onto the floor, where we took our place amidst the dancing couples. It was actually sort of fun — swinging and swaying to the music, Sam's cheek near mine.

"This is a nice song," Sam commented.

"Mmm-hmm."

"Did you ever see the movie?" Sam swung me under his arm.

"Yes. I saw it with Mama."

"Really?" Sam laughed. "I never pictured her as the movie-going type."

I bristled. "What do you mean?"

"Relax." Sam squeezed my hand and smiled. "It wasn't an insult."

"Oh." I pressed my lips together, unable to think of anything else to say. *His eyes are a very nice shade of blue. Funny I never really noticed it when we were little.* Maybe it was because he was now wearing a blue silk shirt.

Sam looked around. "Nice party."

I nodded. "Very nice. The Wilkinsons have a lovely house."

Is this his idea of small talk? It was almost a little funny. *We've never run out of things to talk about before. Why now?*

He glanced at Charlie and Russell, who were doing more staring into each other's eyes than dancing. "They look very happy. Can't say the same about Mrs. Wilkinson."

Russell's mother hovered in a corner, frowning at the couple. Sam laughed. "She has no reason to be worried. Charlie's a sweet girl, despite being a bit of a flirt. She and Russell are good for each other."

I just nodded again and let Sam spin me around, my chiffon skirt swirling around me. The music swelled, and I couldn't help but smile. "Do you think we look at all like Fred and Ginger?"

Sam seemed to consider this for a moment. Then he looked around and lowered his voice. "I could try to sweep you into some fancy dive or lift, if you'd like. But I'm afraid it would draw a great deal of attention from our fellow dancers."

I laughed. "No, this is fine."

The song ended far too soon. Everyone stood and pretended to clap for the gramophone. Mrs. Wilkinson walked into the center of the room and motioned for everyone to stop. "Now, now, that's enough." She smiled. "I'm sure Mr. Astaire would be very pleased." A murmur of laughter filled the room. Mrs. Wilkinson clapped her hands and announced, "Donations for the war effort will be taken in a few minutes, when we all retire to the parlor for some entertainment. Singers, musicians …" She looked around the room eagerly and added. "As well as anyone who wishes to perform for us. Meanwhile, enjoy one last song in your lover's arms." With that, she turned the gramophone back on and returned to her chair.

I left the floor and went back to standing in the doorway. Sam made his way over toward me and together we watched the couples spin around the room.

"So," Sam said after awhile, looking at his hands. "Who was that kid you were so snooty to earlier?"

I didn't take my eyes off the dancers. "What are you talking about?"

"That boy who nearly died of humiliation when you stuck up your nose and said you'd never dance with him."

I smirked. "I didn't say I'd *never* dance with him. I just prefer not to mix with the boys from school."

"Why?" Sam was frowning at me. I looked away.

"They're so … *classless*." I shrugged, glancing at Sam. "You know what I mean."

"But you danced with me."

I laughed. "I didn't have a choice."

Sam bristled. "You could have pushed me away."

"And risk embarrassing myself in front of everyone? I'd never do that." I sighed and fiddled with my skirt. "Besides, I've known you practically forever. And you don't even go to our school, so none of the boys will try to fight with you."

Sam's forehead wrinkled. "Boys fight over you?"

I tilted one side of my mouth and focused on the floor. "It happened in ninth grade, so I haven't talked to any of them since."

"Oh." Sam went silent.

I glanced at him out of the corner of my eye, but couldn't tell what he was thinking. My stomach felt queasy. *Did I offend him?*

Just as I began to open my mouth, people began filing into

139

the parlor, and I was lost in the wave. Mrs. Wilkinson was standing by a piano on an impromptu stage like a queen on her dais, beckoning people toward her.

"Come, come!" she called, excitement in her voice. "You don't expect us to just stand around and talk all night, do you? We need some real entertainment!"

The guests cheered; one fellow even whistled.

Mrs. Wilkinson laughed. "Now, now, settle down." She looked around. "Who will be the first to perform? Don't be shy, youngsters! No one here will judge." She winked.

The room began to hum as people whispered among themselves.

"I'll sing," a timid voice said.

Everyone turned to see Charlie biting her lip, looking nervous. Russell began to clap loudly.

The crowd applauded, nodding their heads. Mrs. Wilkinson's smile faltered only slightly as she swept out her arm grandly. "The stage is yours, Charlie. Do you perform without music?"

"I can." Charlie allowed Russell to help her onto the stage. Once settled she straightened her skirt and chewed on her lip. "Um, do you think 'My Funny Valentine' is okay?"

"If you sing it, it is!" Sam shouted.

"Okay." Charlie giggled. "Here goes …"

As Charlie opened her mouth and began to sing, she changed from stage-struck to confident star. Her eyes brightened and her cheeks flushed, while her honey-blonde curls shone in the candlelight.

She leaned on the piano as she sang, glancing at Russell before shyly looking away. Nearly every young man in the room glared at the lucky man, not that he noticed, I'm sure. He was beaming up at Charlie.

Charlie hit the last note and trailed off, looking nervous again. An awkward silence fell over the room before everyone burst into a thundering applause.

"That was Charlotte Cooper." Mrs. Wilkinson stepped onto the stage and, to my surprise, whispered something in Charlie's ear. Charlie smiled and looked down at Russell, blushing.

"Did you know she could sing?" Sam asked me, clapping loudly.

I shrugged. "Charlie's been my best friend for four years and sometimes I still feel like I don't know that much about her. She's never mentioned singing."

There was another round of applause as Charlie bowed again and scurried off the little stage.

A few more amateur performances followed — a couple second-rate singers and a young dancer with some talent. Mrs. Wilkinson stepped back onto the stage and looked around, wringing her hands as she searched the crowd. "Come now," she said, and I sensed a little desperation in her tone. "Doesn't anyone else want to perform?" The audience was silent.

I looked around. All the young people around me ducked their heads, avoiding Mrs. Wilkinson's stare. I didn't blame them.

Beside me, Sam suddenly stood. "Alcyone Everly can play the piano."

"What?" I whirled around and narrowed my eyes. He avoided my glance.

A disapproving murmur spread through the crowd. Beatrice

stood and frowned at Sam. "Allie doesn't know how. I've been trying to convince her to take lessons for years."

He shook his head. "She can play. Quite beautifully too."

I glared at him. "What are you doing?" I hissed. He shrugged, his eyes wide and innocent.

"Allie, can you play a song?" Mrs. Wilkinson looked confused. I sighed. "Yes."

"Well, will you come up here? I think we're all interested in hearing what you can do. Don't let this fellow's words disappoint us." She waved a glove in Sam's direction.

After giving Sam one last look, I made my way to the piano. I could feel the eyes of nearly one hundred partygoers boring into my back. "Do you have any sheet music?" I whispered to Mrs. Wilkinson.

She shook her head. "I'm sorry, but no." She lowered her voice. "None of us actually know how to play it."

"Oh well ..." I turned to the audience and forced myself to look happy. *I'll just have to play something from memory.* I slid onto the bench and stretched my fingers. Just over the lid of the piano, I could see Beatrice watching me, a mixture of confusion and surprise on her face. I looked down and began to play.

Ravel's "Pavane for a Dead Princess" was the only song I could play by memory. As my fingers slid over the keys, all my years of practicing swept back over me. I smiled slowly—it felt so good to be playing again.

I could hear the audience murmuring, but I didn't look up. Closing my eyes, I let the music take over me.

As the song swelled, my eyes opened. A horrid memory flashed across my mind—the day of Mama's funeral.

It took all I had to finish the song without breaking down. As soon as the last note died down, I stood and briefly bowed before running off the stage and out of the room, leaving the thundering applause behind me.

I burst into the Wilkinson's library and hid as I tried to control my tears. Everything was blurry behind my veil of tears. I buried my face in a bookshelf and sobbed, grabbing a chair for support.

"Allie?" The door creaked open and Beatrice stuck her head in. At the sight of my tear-streaked face, she shut the door behind her and rushed toward me. "Allie, what are you crying for?" She seemed tender as she reached out to smooth back my hair. "That was beautiful! I had no idea ..."

"Stop it!" I jerked my head back and bored my eyes into hers. She winced, and I lowered my voice. "Just stop it." My shoulders shook as I tried to regain my composure. "Please, just leave me alone."

Beatrice puckered her brow. "Allie, I don't understand."

Of course she doesn't. I ducked my head so she couldn't see my tears. A wet drop splashed onto a book beneath me before I could furiously wipe the moisture from my face. "I haven't played," I whispered, "since my mother died. That ... that was the song I played after my mother died ... on the day I had to leave for Maine." I pressed my toe against the ground, concentrating on the waves of pain it sent up my leg.

"Oh, Allie ..." Beatrice's voice softened.

I turned away from her. "I just ... I want to go home."

"Okay." Beatrice nodded. "I can take you home."

I turned my head and stared at her. Her face was illuminated by the candles in the library and the lights from the party behind her.

I shook my head, my stomach dropping. "You can't take me home." I buried my head in a pile of books. *You'll never be able to take me home.*

Chapter 12

The earth has many keys,
Where melody is not
Is the unknown peninsula.
Beauty is nature's fact.

—Emily Dickinson

ere, try this one." Charlie handed me a fresh blueberry and watched my face. I popped the berry into my mouth, and the juice washed over my tongue.

"Delicious."

"I thought so." Charlie smoothed out her dress. "I have a talent for finding fresh berries. I always know *exactly* when they're ripe."

"Then I'm glad to have you around." I bumped her shoulder, nearly causing her to drop her basket.

The warm afternoon sun was beating down on us. Little sweat drops trickled down my back, tickling my skin.

"Do you think Beatrice will make us a pie?" Charlie licked her lips as if she could already taste the sticky sweetness.

The little blueberry patch tucked into the corner of the countryside was bursting with berries. I smiled. "We certainly have enough."

"And I think we've picked plenty." Charlie rocked back on her heels and popped a blueberry into her mouth. I watched as her eyes surveyed the empty countryside, her squinting eyes finally landing on a little red barn at the bottom of the hill. "Have you ever been in there?"

"No." I stood and shaded my eyes. "I don't think there's anything in there."

"You mean it's abandoned?" Charlie practically shivered with excitement. "Come on, Allie, let's act like little girls and go exploring. It'll be fun." She wrapped her fingers around my arm. "Follow me."

I dropped my basket and ran through the tall grass behind Charlie, trailing my fingers through the golden waves surrounding me. For the first time in many days I felt alive and happy and full.

She skidded to a stop in front of the barn. It was covered in cobwebs and dust, the cracked windows letting in only slits of sunlight and fresh air.

I glanced over my shoulder, to where the car was parked at the top of the hill. "Do you think it's okay up there?"

Charlie shrugged. "There's no one around for miles. Come on, let's go inside." She pushed open the barn door with a *creak* and giggled.

A cloud of dust rained down on our heads as the heavy doors swung open. I squealed and jumped back as a spider slowly spun down from its elevated web.

I leaped again when Charlie squeezed my arm. "Allie, it's so creepy."

Steeling myself, I stepped inside the barn and looked around. A musty smell hung in the air. Dust fell from the rafters, and old piles of hay were clustered around the ground. But the sun shone through the peeling beams in the most peculiar way, casting an eerie light over the large room.

"I like it," I decided. "It's a bit spooky, but also very charming."

I settled down on a bale of ancient hay and propped my chin in my hands. Charlie sat in front of me and smiled slowly. "Tell me a secret," she said.

My mouth twitched. "Hmmm … a secret." I traced my lips with my finger, thinking. "I never knew how to swim until this summer."

Charlie frowned. "That's not a secret. I've known that for years, and I already figured out that Sam boy taught you how to swim." She straightened. "Tell me a secret about Sam."

I gulped. "What do you want to know?"

"Something about him you've never told anyone before." Charlie shifted on the hay. "Something good."

"Um, okay." I looked up at the sunlight peeking through the rafters, illuminating the dust that danced through the air. The room seemed to sit still — the silence stretching on. As I searched my memory for a secret about Sam, a piece of hair fell over my eye. I blew it off and squirmed.

"One year for my birthday, Sam gave me a set of chalks." I bit my lip, holding back a smile. My voice softened. "It was the best gift I ever got." I remembered how I received the gift, and all at once I wished I could go back in time and change how I'd treated him.

"That's not much of a secret," Charlie said, annoyed. "I was hoping for something a little more … exciting." She wiggled her blonde eyebrows at me.

I lifted my chin and shrugged. "Doesn't matter. He's a boring boy, anyway. Never did anything worth sharing." I shoved away the voice inside my head that argued otherwise. "Tell me a secret of your own."

A shy smile crept across Charlie's face. "Well, I do have a *little* secret."

"What about?"

Charlie giggled and wrapped her arms around herself. "I heard Russell talking to his mother the other night." She sighed. "He complimented her on her shoes …"

I snorted, then coughed to cover it up.

"Then he told her he thought I was pretty and smart and wonderful." Charlie glanced at me pointedly. "Those were his exact words: 'pretty, smart, and wonderful.' Mrs. Wilkinson said she couldn't disagree." She fiddled with a piece of hay. "Do you think he likes me?"

I resituated myself so I lay on my stomach. "Of course he does."

"Then why doesn't he tell me?"

I laughed. "He does — with everything but words. Don't worry, Charlie, I think he'll be around for a good while longer." I wrapped a dark piece of hair around my finger.

Charlie smiled, looking down at her hands. She rubbed her ring finger and grew quiet, her bright face dimming. "Annie

Merimont still wears her engagement ring. I saw her at the grocery store the other day and there it was, plain as the nose on my face."

My mouth twitched. "Well, it's only been a few months."

"Still." Charlie rolled onto her stomach and looked at me. "Annie thought Gerry would be around for a long time too. And he died eight weeks before the wedding."

I shifted, uncomfortable. "Charlie, it's a time of war. That kind of thing happens. Russell's not going anywhere. He'll be fine. We all will."

Charlie let out a little sigh and sat up again. Shafts of light peeked through the rafters, illuminating the dust floating in the air. "I know, I know. It's just..." She trailed off and turned toward me. "I don't know how things are going to turn out. No one really does. Not us, not Germany, not Japan, not England …" She began chewing a fingernail, then caught herself. "I'm just starting to think stuff matters. Like Russell matters now. He's not just some boy who I want to date for a while and then hurt and throw away. I've dated every boy in town. And Russell's never even thought about any other girl."

I snorted. Charlie shook her head. "I mean, other than you or me." She wrinkled her nose. "It's just … I'm thinking about tomorrow. And the next day. And all the days after that." She shrugged, still looking as cute and innocent as the day I met her. "I don't want to be alone."

Charlie Cooper being philosophical? I lowered my brow. "Why would you be alone, Charlie? You're beautiful and sweet and lovable. You don't have to worry about that."

A tiny pucker appeared on her forehead. "What if … What

if it's not enough? Maybe being pretty and sweet and good isn't good enough in the end." Her blue eyes clouded over in thought. "The Japanese could come and kill us all any day. They could drop a bomb on us right this very instant! And then ..." She shook her head slowly. "Then what would we do? Would being pretty and nice be enough?" She looked ready to cry. "What would happen next?"

I pulled myself upright and pushed the thought away. "There is no God. It doesn't really matter."

Charlie shrugged her small shoulders, causing hair to tumble off her back. "Can't be sure. Not completely." She blew the hay off her finger and watched it fall to the ground. "I guess we'll never be sure until it's over."

I stared at the fallen hay until my eyes went out of focus. *I guess we'll never be sure until it's over ...*

I wrapped my arms around myself, suddenly feeling cold. *Could I be sure?* What if even I was wrong about God and heaven? What could I be sure of then?

Charlie shook her hair and giggled. "Maybe I'm being silly. I sure feel silly. Sitting here thinking all wisely with hay in my hair."

I rolled my eyes. "It isn't the best place in the world to be philosophical. Rats could get us at any moment."

"Let's go." Charlie grabbed my hand in her slender, pale one and pulled me toward the door.

* * * * *

I turned the light on in Beatrice's library and looked around. I hadn't been in the room for four years — shunning it ever since the day of my arrival.

The design seemed practically untouched since I'd been in there last. A few added shelves here and there and a small reading desk, but nothing outrageously new.

I settled behind the little desk and ran my fingers over the smooth mahogany wood. It was lovely. My skin crawled as I fought down the urge to jump up and run, my mind replaying the thought, *This is Beatrice's desk, not yours.*

Beatrice once said it could be mine, didn't she? She said it could be "our house."

I pulled out my notebook and opened to a new page, smoothing it down as I reached for a writing instrument. Pressing the cold pen to my lips, my hand paused over the paper. *How did that poem start off?*

The pen seemed to fly of its own accord over the paper, swirling and looping as it crafted line after line. I closed my eyes and remembered how it felt to be spinning across the dance floor "cheek to cheek."

Where is Sam right now? I bit my lip and glanced out the window. Maybe he was outside, standing on the beach and watching the waves.

I paused only a second before pushing away from the desk and heading out the side door. *I'd like to ask him if—*

I halted mid-step. The beach was empty, with the exception of a few laughing children and their parents. I sighed and stuck my notebook under my arm, shuffling back toward the house. *I didn't really want to see him anyway.*

A whistle pierced the air, sounding off a familiar tune. I whirled around; the sound was coming from Rachel Piper's backyard.

I ran down the beach and up the hill, my thoughts flying as fast as my feet. I skidded to a stop in the middle of Rachel's yard. Sam was sitting under an apple tree, whistling to himself while he whittled away at a piece of wood.

He looked up in surprise. "Hi."

"Hi." My lungs were screaming. I crumpled onto the ground in front of Sam and placed a hand on my heaving chest. A smile twitched on my mouth as he frowned at me in bewilderment. "Daydreaming?" I asked.

His eyes warmed and he shook his head, holding up the wood. "Whittling."

"What is it? A boat?" I reached out for the lumpy project, puzzling as I turned it over in my hands. I looked up to see Sam smiling wryly.

"No, it's a pencil."

A snort escaped my nose. I clamped a hand over my face to hide my giggles. "A pencil?" I finally managed. I bit my lip, suppressing more laughter. "How long —" I coughed and forced a serious expression. "How long have you been carving?"

Sam snatched the wood out of my hand and glared at me. "Long enough to know how to make a pencil." He held his project with an air of wounded pride.

My stomach hurt from holding back my amusement. "It's ... it's ..." *It's horrendous, that's what it is.*

Sam was watching me with a frown on his face. He held up his pencil and studied it. "It's not that bad, is it?"

I nodded. "Yes," I gasped. "I don't mean to hurt you, but it is."

Sam rolled his eyes and threw the hunk of wood over his

shoulder. "Oh well." He glanced at me and smirked. "I guess it was kind of ugly."

My laughter stopped, and I looked over to where the pencil had landed. "Can I keep it?"

"What?"

"Would you give it to me?"

Sam pushed a hand through his hair. "Yeah, I guess." He stood and dusted off his pants before picking up the pencil and laying it on my lap. "A pencil, my lady."

"Thank you." I turned the ugly carving over in my hands. "It's beautiful."

Sam chuckled and shook his head, settling back on the ground. "Glad you think something you professed hideous is nice to look at."

I smiled at him before looking back down at the gift. *It really is a rather nice pencil, I suppose. It might work for writing and sketching, if I can get the lead put in it somehow.* I bit back a grin. *I wonder if Sam even thought that far ahead.*

Sam leaned back against the apple tree and folded his arms behind his head. "So what are you doing here?"

"I live with Beatrice Lovell. Her house is right over there." I pointed across the water.

Now it was Sam's turn to laugh. He rolled his eyes. "Not Maine. My yard."

"Don't know. You're always so *surprising*." My mouth twitched. "Guess I just wanted to see what you were up to, that's all." I moved over to Sam so I could better see the large, elegant house in front of us. "Nice place you have here." I crossed my arms across my chest and squinted at noonday sun reflecting off the many windows. "You know I've been living within a stone's throw from your aunt Rachel for three years now, and I've still never set foot inside her house." I frowned at Sam. "Is she just snobby or does she genuinely not like me?"

Sam shrugged. "She hasn't had anyone over as long as I've been here. Well, other than the ladies' knitting circle that meets on Tuesdays. But even then I'm sent outside or to my room. I think she considers me like a dog or something. Nice to look at, but a bother to clean up after." His eyes suddenly fell on my journal. "What are you working on?"

"A poem." I reddened.

"Mind if I see?" He reached over and snatched it up before I could fight him off.

My stomach grew hot as I watched his eyes scan the poem. *It's just a load of silliness, that's all. He won't think I'm serious ... will he?*

The seconds ticked by slowly. I looked down at the grass — then back at Sam. He was still reading the poem, his lips parted in concentration. Finally, he looked up and placed the notebook back on my lap. My stomach flipped.

Sam shifted and picked at one of the buds on the branch above us. "That was beautiful, Allie."

"Really?" I looked at him carefully and shut the notebook. "It was nothing."

"No, it was talent." Sam looked down and met my eyes. "Have you ever considered publishing a book of poems?"

"What?" I shook my head and pushed the notebook away from me. "No way. Not in a million years. No."

Sam laughed softly. "You might be surprised. You're better

than you think, Alcyone Everly. And one day you'll know it."
His blue eyes softened as he smiled at me.

"Thanks," I whispered, clutching the notebook to my chest.
My head felt dizzy. Only the sound of the crashing waves could
be heard above the silence.

"So, did you want a cup of tea?" Sam asked, standing. He
helped me up and shook the apple blossoms out of his hair.

"No, thanks. I need to be getting back." I shifted on the
balls of my feet.

Sam grinned and picked a pink flower out of my hair. "You
look like a fairy princess."

I brushed the dirt off my white dress, trying to ignore his
proximity. "I should have known better than to sit on the ground."

He shrugged. "Just scrub it with soap and water. No harm
done."

"Thanks." I picked up my notebook, feeling awkward.
"Okay, well ... I guess I'll see you later."

He nodded. "Tell Charlie and Russell I said hello."

I tucked the notebook under my arm and turned to go, running down the hill and to the oceanfront. *Well that was*——

"Allie!"

I turned to see Sam rushing after me. He slowed down and
proclaimed, "I forgot to mention that Aunt Rachel wished to cor-
dially invite you to lunch tomorrow afternoon. In fact, you saved
me a trip to your house later today. I'll tell her you'll be there at
noon." He winked before turning and walking back up the hill.

I sighed to the heavens and trudged home. Beatrice was sitting in the library, perusing an old book. She looked up expec-
tantly as I opened the door.

"Oh, there you are, Allie." She tilted her head. "Where have you been?"

I shut the door behind me. "At Rachel Piper's house. I was talking with Sam Carroll, who invited me to lunch tomorrow."

"Did he really?" Beatrice shook her head slightly and laughed softly. "Well that was very nice of him. I have to admit, he is a strange young ruffian."

I blew a piece of hair out of my eyes. "You have no idea." I peered down at my notebooks, noticing large fingerprints were visible on the faded cover. I tucked away a smile in the corner of my mouth. *Is Sam right? Do I have talent?*

"Penny for your thoughts," Beatrice said, rising to arrange the tea tray.

I placed the notebook on the desk, feeling light as air. "I was just thinking that high tea is *positively medieval.*"

✻ ✽ ✻ ✽ ✻

Someone knocked on my bedroom door. I looked up from the desk. "Come in."

Beatrice poked her head in the doorway. "I was just wondering what you were going to wear to lunch at Rachel Piper's house." She paused and twisted her hands. "Rachel is a very elegant woman."

"Oh, that." I rolled my eyes. "That's not for a few hours yet." I bent my head back over my journal, scribbling away.

"What are you talking about, Allie?" Beatrice pointed at the clock. "It's already eleven thirty."

My head flew up. I shut the journal with a bang, hopping up from the desk. I glanced at the clock — sure enough, Beatrice was right. "I didn't realize it was getting so late."

"A girl in disarray's thoughts are far away." Beatrice leaned in the doorway, then hesitated. "You're always writing in that journal of yours." Her eyes searched over the journal from a distance. "What do you write about?" she asked, her voice soft.

My first reaction was to stare at her. I'd considered this a taboo subject. She never asked me about my writing and I never offered any insight. That's the way things were between us. I spread my arms over the journal, blocking it from her view. "Nothing."

Beatrice's face crumpled, only for a moment. Then she smoothed it out quickly until I could see no more of the crinkles. The smile she gave me was distant and polite. "Oh. I see."

My cheeks grew hot. "What I mean is … it's private." The words seemed jumbled in my mouth, unable to come out. "I'd let you … I mean, I just think … I don't want anyone to …"

"Oh," Beatrice said again. But this time the word seemed a little brighter. "Perhaps one day you'll let me look at it."

I grabbed the notebook and shoved it into my dresser, my back turned to Beatrice. My hands were shaking as I pushed the drawer shut with a slam. "It's about my mother."

Beatrice was silent. It took me several seconds before I had enough bravery to face her again, and when I did she was staring at me with an unreadable expression on her face.

"You write about her?" she finally asked.

My face stayed frozen in the same half-fearful, half-defiant face.

But Beatrice just nodded. "That's good." She licked her lips. "She must have been quite the woman."

I nodded. "She was. She …" I took a deep breath. "She was

the nicest person I've ever known. She cared about people. Kind of like …" I glanced at Beatrice, who was listening intently. *Kind of like you.*

The thought shocked and repulsed me. How could I have ever …

I looked down. *No, nothing like Beatrice. She couldn't be like Beatrice.*

And yet I could almost see it. The quiet pride. The love for all things beautiful and interesting. The way they both seemed to understand when to push things with me and when to let them go.

The only difference was the religion. Beatrice would never be like my mother in that respect.

The room fell silent. The conversation was over.

Beatrice cleared her throat. "Well, I came to see what you were wearing, and I haven't seen it yet."

I frowned. "I'll probably just put on the first dress in my closet." I'd already made sure it was the deep-blue dress with the lace collar.

Beatrice gripped the doorway and gulped. "Well, then you do that." Her smile was strained. "Just try to be appropriate." She looked around the room one last time, her gaze resting on the dresser. Then she spun on her heel and shut the door behind her.

I stared at the space she'd occupied. Had Beatrice really just stood there? Had I really told her what I spent never-ending hours writing about in my journal?

I groaned and fell back onto the bed. I didn't like to talk about Mama—least of all to Beatrice.

Maybe Beatrice … maybe she'd understand Mama. She sometimes had Mama's light in her eyes when she was happy or thankful. Or when she looked at Irene. And … me?

I gulped down the bile in my throat. No, Beatrice would never be to me what she was to Irene. She'd never understand Mama or be anything like her. She'd never know about the little cuts on Mama's hands from the rose thorns she trimmed. Or about the little tremors she'd get in her voice when she read aloud an exciting battle scene or a touching poem.

My fingers curled up and gripped the blanket on the bed. I stroked the soft pillow.

Something ricocheted against my window, making a loud *ping*. I jumped up and grabbed my pillow in defense. I slowly walked toward the window and looked down.

Sam was smiling up at me. He waved and motioned for me to stick my head out.

I groaned and opened the window. "Don't people generally do this at night?" I called down.

Sam just grinned. "I got hungry, and Aunt Rachel said I could come and get you. So come on!"

I tried to keep my face angry, but failed. "Let me put on something nice and I'll be right down."

Sam straightened his collar. "I'll wait all day for that."

With a laugh, I shut the window and grabbed the deep-blue dress out of the wardrobe.

* * * * *

"So …" Miss Rachel's eyes roamed over me like twin searchlights as she raised a fork to her mouth. She raised an eyebrow. "I understand you've known Samuel for quite some time."

I squirmed in my antique chair. "Yes, I have. Since we were children."

"Strange, Samuel never mentioned you before this summer." Miss Rachel narrowed her eyes at me.

My palms began to sweat. I pushed around the peas on my plate. "Well, I ..."

"We haven't seen each other in years, Aunt Rachel," Sam jumped in. "It was quite a pleasant surprise to meet Allie here this summer, after having not seen her in over three years."

I gave a thin smile and looked down at my plate. The china pattern was centuries old—an English vine curling around a yellow rose. I stuck a piece of meat with my fork and forced it down my throat.

"Well, Alcyone," Miss Rachel said, stretching out every syllable of my name, "what do you think of my home?"

I looked around and gulped. It was certainly the most elegant house I had ever been in. A large crystal chandelier hung over my head, dripping with antique glass and gold. Priceless paintings were pinned to the walls, and rich red wallpaper lined the room. We reclined on mahogany wingbacked chairs, and were served on sterling silver trays.

"It's a beautiful home," I said. "Very elegant."

"Thank you." Miss Rachel beamed, looking like a gratified bird with her feathers fluffed out. "I spent years getting it this way." She smoothed down her white hair and poured more tea into my cup.

I caught Sam watching me from the other side of the table. I widened my eyes at him and looked down at my piping-hot tea.

"Would you like to retire to the parlor?" Miss Rachel asked.

"I have a nice piano you are welcome to try out. Samuel tells me you play nicely."

I blushed. "Oh, no, I …"

"Come now! No protests!" Miss Rachel pushed herself out of her seat with a groan, pressing a hand on her back. Sam moved to help her, but she waved him off. "You entertain our guest for a few moments while I clear the table. I'll be right there."

Sam smiled at me, then gave a little bow. "Shall we retire to the parlor?"

I followed him into a smaller, less formal room. There were several chairs gathered in a circle, and a large piano standing alone in the corner. I ran my fingers over the instrument and felt a wave of bliss pass over me. "I feel like I'm in a Victorian fairy tale."

"It can give you that effect." Sam pulled at his necktie and smirked. "She's got me dressed up like an English gentlemen at all times."

I looked back down at the piano. It was white, and nearly twice the size of Mama's. "It's a lovely piano."

When I glanced back up, Sam was watching me. "You should play it. I would enjoy hearing you, unpressured and free." He looked down at his hands. "I shouldn't have put you in the position I did at the Wilkinson's party."

My stomach hurt at the sight of his sorry face. I shrugged and tried to smile nonchalantly. "I'll play for you, if you want. Besides"—I motioned at the large stack of sheet music sitting on top of the piano—"I haven't had this kind of selection in years."

I fingered through the selections and pulled out a faded paper. "Do you know Debussy's 'Reverie'?"

Sam shook his head and leaned on the piano. "No, but I'd love to hear your rendition."

I pulled back the bench and settled down. After smoothing the sheet music out in front of me, I began to play.

The song had only happy memories — memories of warm summer days spent practicing the piano and glancing out the little window where Mama was hanging up fluttering clothes in the sun.

My fingers stumbled once, as I fought to recognize the right notes. My heart felt like soaring, though, as the music rose and fell. I trailed off the last keys and smiled, looking up at Sam.

He stood and clapped, grinning like a fool. "Marvelous!"

Miss Rachel stood also, from the loveseat in the back, and nodded. "That was lovely, Alcyone. Samuel's praise was more than justified."

I blushed and grabbed the sheet music, placing it back on top of the stack. "It was one of the last songs Mama taught me," I explained, tracing a finger over the printed notes.

"Does Beatrice have a piano?" Sam asked, settling on the sofa.

I sat across from him and shook my head. "No, though she talked about buying one a few years ago. She didn't know I played until I performed at the Wilkinsons.'"

An awkward silence fell over us all as Miss Rachel examined me closely again. "That's a pretty dress," she finally said.

I glanced down at the dark-blue fabric. "Thank you."

Sam leaned forward, his hair falling on his forehead. "I

never asked you how yours and Charlie's blueberry excursion was, Allie."

"It was fine, thank you." I smiled and squirmed under Miss Rachel's stare. *Honestly, couldn't she look somewhere else once in a while?* "Have you heard any new developments from the war front?" I asked.

Miss Rachel's gaze turned cold. She placed her hands in her lap primly. "The war in Europe is not worth discussing in my household."

I lowered by brow. "It would seem to me worth discussing in every American household."

Miss Rachel's glare pierced through me. "I do not support innocent boys being slaughtered on the battlefield for a worthless cause."

Sam bristled, inching forward in his chair. "That cause is the defense of our freedom. If those brave men didn't step up and defy those who would seek to hold them back, we might not enjoy the freedoms we have today. Those men fight for *America*."

"Those *boys* fight for themselves." Miss Rachel's eyes burned with a cold fire, stopping my breath short.

Sam's voice rose with equal heat. "Those men fight for their country and you know it!"

"I agree," I said softly.

The silence that now hung over us seemed ten times more awkward than before. I glanced at Sam to see him staring at his hands. He looked up and tried to smile at me.

"Allie, I—"

"I should be going," I said, interrupting him. I stood and curt-seyed to Miss Rachel, feeling foolish and clumsy. "Beatrice will be expecting me at home. Thank you for the lovely lunch. It was …" I trailed off. *It was what? "Lovely"?* I felt like kicking myself.

Sam stood as well. "I'll walk you home if you want."

"No, I can get there myself." I infused my voice with mirth. "It's just on the other side of the beach."

Miss Rachel held out a hand to me regally. "It was a pleasure to meet you, Alcyone Everly. I do hope I will have the joy again in the near future."

I nodded and forced a smile. "Me too. Perhaps Beatrice and I will return the favor." Then I turned and opened the side door, running toward the water as soon as my feet hit soil.

I stopped when I reached the beach and pulled off my shoes, letting the sand tickle my toes. The warm breeze caressed my face, cooling my heated thoughts.

Who is she to say the war is a foolish, selfish cause? She doesn't have a patriotic bone in her body!

I clenched my fist and slowly released it, breathing in. *Easy does it, Allie.*

I glanced back up at Rachel Piper's house on the hill. Someone was watching me from a window. *Sam.* I smiled at him and gave a little wave. He waved back, and the curtain fell into place.

I went on my way, smiling as I walked. The sand had never felt nicer beneath my feet.

* * * * *

"Allie, did you hang the clothes up on the line?"

I looked up from my book to see Beatrice standing in the doorway of my room, frowning. She glanced at what was in my hands and rolled her eyes. "Allie," The hint of a laugh lingered behind her voice. "How many times have I reminded you to take care of your responsibilities before you lose yourself in all those books for yours? I've always said that a girl who does chores has a future that soars."

I could hear her laugh fading down the hallway. I sighed and placed the Emily Dickinson volume on my nightstand. *What was the real world created for anyway? The pretend world is so much nicer.*

I picked up the basket of laundry and headed to the yard. *Darned chores.*

The screen door slammed behind me, causing a slight breeze to tickle the back of my legs. The grass felt warm beneath my bare toes as I reached up to pin a light-blue dress on the wire line.

I closed my eyes and inhaled the fresh scent of the clean laundry. *When I was little, hanging laundry was my favorite thing in the world to do.* I chewed my lip. *It was Mama's too.*

Someone shouted, breaking my reverie. I looked up, but there was no one on the beach. My brow pinched. *I thought I heard—*

There it was again—yelling. This time there was no doubt about it.

I slowly stood, letting the laundry drop into the basket. The sound was coming from Rachel Piper's house.

The soft sand pillowed the thumping of my feet as I crept up the beach. I stood in Rachel's yard, my lips pinched together. *This is silly. Maybe I should . . .*

"What do you know?" Sam was shouting.

I tip-toed across the yard and under the apple tree, wrapping my body against the bark for shelter. From my hiding place I could see the parlor window. The figures of Sam and Rachel Piper were facing each other, each silhouette looking hostile.

Rachel's voice rose as she took a step toward Sam. "You had better write her back or else I'll ..."

"Or you'll what? Send me away too?" Sam flung out an arm. "You think that sending me to another aunt or cousin or grandparent is going to solve anything? You think that she'll honestly love me more if she doesn't see me?" Sam turned his back to his aunt, his shoulders visibly shaking. His voice lowered, and I couldn't hear him anymore.

I felt like a snoop, standing in the middle of Sam's garden, listening in on his heated conversations. Checking to make sure no one was at the windows, I turned on my heel and pushed away from the apple tree, hoping to sneak away without notice.

"Allie?"

My heart froze. I turned around slowly, my face already flushing.

Sam was standing in front of me, a look of disbelief on his face. He took a step forward, and I noticed tear streaks were visible on his cheeks. "What are you doing here?"

What am I doing here? I opened my mouth, but no words came out. I twisted the hem of my skirt and stepped back, feeling wretched. "I ... I heard the voices and I thought ..." Each word cracked as it left my throat. "I'm sorry. I shouldn't have come."

I faced Beatrice's house once again and began to run down the beach, heat spreading behind my eyelids. But it was only a matter of seconds before Sam was beside me, grabbing my shoulders.

"Allie, wait."

I stopped and faced Sam. He gulped, sticking his hands in his pockets. Now that we were closer, I saw his eyes were puffy and his hair disheveled.

I bit my lip and waited for him to speak. The hush between us seemed to stretch on forever, punctuated by the squawking seagulls above us.

"You heard?" he whispered, avoiding my eyes.

I shrugged. "I only heard a little."

He frowned and rubbed his face, looking like he was about to throw up.

My own stomach began to roil. "You don't have to—"

"No." The word came forcefully, made more powerful by the look in Sam's eyes. "I just ... I just didn't want anyone to know. And, I mean, you of all people." He kicked the sand, and I realized he was still wearing a pajama shirt.

Well, no wonder. It can't be past ten in the morning.

"You want to go for a walk?" Sam asked, squinting at me. I followed him down the beach—I was almost afraid to leave him alone. Sam kept his eyes down until we had reached a point where his house was no longer visible. Then he took a shaky breath and stopped to face me.

"Okay. Here's what happened." Sam's eyes shot to mine. "Everything I told you ... about my brother dying and my parent's dissention toward the military ... all that is true. But Robbie's death isn't what made me leave home. It was because—" Sam's shoulders slumped. "The day after Robbie's funeral, I signed up to join the army. When my mother found out, well, she was mad as a hornet. She stomped down to the office and argued with the staff until she was blue in the face. And she won, in the end. They denied my claims of volunteering, and my mother made it pretty clear that nothing like that was ever going to happen again."

Sam began to walk, taking long, even strides. I strained my shorter legs to keep up with him.

"Mother and I began to argue. Over little things. She thought I was an ungrateful ingrate; I thought she was an overbearing tyrant." Sam jammed a hand through his hair. "One thing led to another and then it was over. I finally made the decision to come and live with Aunt Rachel. I needed some ..." He glanced at me out of the side of his eye. "Well, I heard you were here and I wanted to see you again."

I stared at him in silence for a moment. If I hadn't just heard it, I never would have believed it: Sam Carroll—arguing with someone? Sam Carroll—holding hostile feelings toward someone? *Not sweet Sam Carroll.* And he'd never shown a hint of this turmoil around me.

Sam was watching me, an uncertain look on his face. I shifted. *He must want me to say something.*

I racked my brains for the right words. "Why?"

Sam frowned. "What?" I'd already said it—I couldn't take it back. I shrugged and asked again. "Why? Why did you argue with your mother? Why did you argue with your aunt?" The questions kept pouring out of my mouth. "Why did you argue with anyone at all?" I frowned. "It doesn't seem like you."

Sam fell silent, but he began to walk again. "I don't know," he muttered after awhile. "I guess it really just got to me. I mean, she was treating me like a child. If Robbie was man enough to make his own decisions and die for his country, then so was I." He slowed, and caught my eye. "I'm eighteen, you know. I'm not a kid anymore."

"Yeah, but does your mom realize that?"

"What do you mean?"

I paused to pick up a seashell. I turned the shell over and examined the swirls. "When Mama was sick, she used to forget how old I was almost constantly. One minute I'd be her protector and provider; the next minute I was a helpless little child, dependent on her care." I tucked the shell into my pocket and smiled at Sam. "I guess all parents are like that, though. They don't really see time the same way we do. You are your mother's baby, and you always will be, whether you're eighteen or eighty."

Sam sighed, his blue eyes clouding over. "I just don't want to talk to her. I don't want to answer her letters, or ring her up on the telephone, or see her face again. At least for now."

"Oh." My mouth quivered. I focused on a spot on Sam's pajama shirt, just above his shoulder. "You know ..." My eyes blurred. "You should be thankful you have a mother. I wish every day that—" I lowered my voice to a whisper. "I'd do anything to talk to my mother again."

Sam reached out and touched my shoulder. "Well, you have Beatrice. And she cares about you, I can tell."

I swallowed. It was true. Beatrice cared about me every bit as much as Mama and she even ... My mouth went dry. *What am I thinking?* "Beatrice is not my mother," I said, more to myself than him. I flinched away from his touch.

He dropped his hand and stuck it in his pocket. "Sorry." He squinted at me, looking ashamed.

My mouth twitched. "It's okay. I didn't mean to react like that. It's just …" I lowered my eyes. "I don't like to think about it." *Because you know what you've always thought about Beatrice isn't true.* I kicked at the sand. *If it isn't true, then I don't have reason to fight anymore.*

I took a ragged breath. "Well, I guess we're in the same boat. We're both stuck in someone else's house and we both just want to be free to make our own decisions."

"Yeah." Sam grinned. "I guess we kind of need each other."

My stomach tingled. *This is bad. This is not what it should be.* I frowned fiercely, turning to walk back toward the houses. "No, I don't think so. I don't think so at all."

* * * * *

I licked my sugary, lemonade-soaked lips and leaned my head against the porch post. The sky was bluer than the ocean—a light, jewel-toned blue. *What would it be like to wear a necklace made of sky stones?* I tossed the idea around in my mind, smiling to myself.

A beat-up truck pulled in the driveway, slinging gravel. It rolled to a stop, and Sam stuck his mussed head out of the window. "Hi."

"Hi."

He motioned to the truck. "Want to go for a ride? I thought we could do your mom a favor and pick up some stuff from town."

"She's not—"

"I know, I know." Sam waved an arm. "She's not your mom."

A smile twitched in the corner of my mouth. "I was going

to say she's not home right now. But I can telephone her at Mrs. Wilkinson's house." I pushed open the screen door and went inside, putting my empty glass in the sink before calling Beatrice.

"Come on!" Sam shouted.

"Can I at least put on my shoes?" The horn sounded in answer, so I grabbed the footwear I'd left on the porch and ran down the gravel driveway, sliding as gracefully as possible into the passenger seat. As the vehicle shifted into gear, I patted the door. "This thing looks like it belongs in Tennessee, not Maine."

Sam smiled, pulling out of the driveway. "It's been a long time since you've been in Tennessee. You might be surprised." He headed toward town. "Well? What's on the list?"

"She needs baking powder and paint thinner."

"Paint thinner?" Sam exclaimed.

"I think we're painting the shed or something."

"Oh."

I didn't look at him, staring out the window instead. Quaint New England houses sped past us, surrounded by splotches of green. *It's been a long time since you've been in Tennessee ...* "Has it changed?" I asked in a low voice.

"What? Tennessee?" He gripped the steering wheel. "No."

My heart pinched. *Those beautiful Tennessee hills ...* I wiped my eye with a sleeve and hoped it was discreet. "Well, I'm glad."

Sam nodded. "It's good to know some things don't change."

A sudden thought flashed across my mind. I opened my mouth, almost afraid to ask the question. "And my house?" I whispered. "Have you seen it lately?"

Sam turned and met my eyes as we rolled to a stop before a stop sign. "I used to drive past it every day. It hasn't changed much."

The next words were hard to say. "Is someone living there now?"

He cleared his throat. "Yeah. But they're good people. They've still got your cat, Daphne, and she's fat as can be. I still give her a good head rub when I run across her in the woods sometimes. She seems pretty happy."

His eyes suddenly seemed like gleaming sapphires. I closed my eyes and forced myself to swallow. "Thanks."

A car behind us honked. Sam looked away and muttered something under his breath, glancing over his shoulder. "You're supposed to stop at stop signs," he explained, as if I was the angry one. "It's the law."

I focused on the window so Sam couldn't see me laughing to myself. Within minutes we rolled into town and pulled up in front of the hardware store. With some effort I pushed the truck door open and hopped out, slamming it behind me.

When we reached the shop, Sam made a point of rushing ahead and holding open the entrance, and for once didn't bow. Little bells jingled as we entered.

The man behind the counter spotted Sam and nodded, motioning for us to come to the front. "Good day, sir. How can I help you?"

"We need paint thinner. For her." Sam jerked his head in my direction.

I pressed a hand against my mouth, holding back a smile. *Does he realize how ridiculous he looks when he's trying to look tough?*

Sam glared at me and turned back to the clerk. The man shook his head. "Sorry, all out."

"What?" we both asked at the same time. I glanced at Sam. He set his jaw and leaned against the counter. "Where can we get some?"

The clerk shrugged. "There's a little farm outside of town that usually carries paint. I can give them a telephone call if you like."

Sam nodded, and the man disappeared in the back of the store. I strummed my fingers on the counter, the smile again threatening to break through.

"They have some in their barn," the clerk said, coming back to the desk. "Here is the address." He handed Sam a piece of paper.

Sam looked at it and winced slightly. "Thanks." He turned and paused in the doorway, looking back over his shoulder. "Oh, and can we have some baking powder?" After he paid for the powder, we left the shop, and I tried to get a glimpse of the paper Sam was holding.

"Sorry," he muttered as we climbed into the truck. "This looks like another half-hour drive."

"That's okay. I'm in no hurry to get back."

He started up the engine and pulled out of town. Once the buildings were behind us, the open countryside seemed to engulf us in pools of green. I leaned my forehead against the glass, content. "I haven't been driving out here in a while."

"It's pretty," Sam said.

I nodded, and let the silence carry us for a while. "Remember when we were little?" I asked, grinning. "We used to go out to the hills — or, rather, you followed me out to the hills when I went there to draw. I used to think you were in love with me."

Sam smiled. "I was. Madly."

I rolled my eyes. "And what, pray tell, made you so utterly crazy about me? Was it my scabby legs? My scowling brow?" I wiggled my eyebrows.

Sam shook his head. "No, I think it was more your mystery."

The giggle died in my throat. I ran my finger along the seat, tracing little circles. "What do you mean?"

Sam pressed his lips together and kept his eyes on the road. "You were always so ... reclusive. The kids at school used to call you a witch or something, and say your mom was possessed and you had cast a spell on her." He cracked a small smile and glanced at me. "I didn't believe in your ability to cast spells until the first time I snuck over to your house and watched you. I think I was five years old. And I was in love from that day on."

"Really? Oh, that's so sweet." I elbowed his ribs. "Tell me more."

He raised his eyebrows. "You really are so humble."

"Oh, come on."

He chuckled. "Okay. I also thought you were pretty. And I thought you played the piano well. And your garden was the most beautiful heaven on earth."

"It was not." I twirled a piece of hair around my finger, enjoying the conversation.

Sam glanced at me. "Was too. And you were always writing in that little journal of yours. I used to imagine what you wrote in it, and always thought up the wildest stuff." His voice lowered a little. "You were also so kind to your mother. That day we went on a picnic and she ..." He trailed off and began humming, strumming his fingers on the steering wheel. "Well, it was a long time ago."

I looked away and tried to ignore my beating heart. The green grass whizzed by, blurring in my mind.

We pulled in front of a little homestead in the middle of the countryside, which Charlie would have squealed over. Even I had to admit it was cute.

"Stay here." Sam swung out the door and headed for the barn. Within minutes, he was hauling back a tin of thinner and two cans of paint, placing them in the bed of the truck. "All taken care of," he said, climbing back into the seat.

I turned and frowned. "Sam, how much did those cost?"

He shrugged. "Not much."

"Seriously. I have to pay you back."

He shook his head and smiled. "No need. I like Beatrice too. I mean ... We both like Beatrice. Her shed is really pretty, but it could stand some paint, and I figured I might as well pick out a nice color for the two of you while we're here."

"Sam, I can't ..."

He held up a hand. "Don't talk about it anymore."

We drove until the farm was a little spot in the distance, and then not visible at all. The lush fields surrounded us; the long grasses swayed in the wind. I leaned toward the open window and smiled, feeling the wind on my cheek. My dark hair whipped my eyes.

The air smelled sweet — like sunshine and flowers and ... smoke? I wrinkled my nose. "Sam, do you smell something burning?" The truck began to sputter, smoke pouring from the hood. Sam groaned and pulled over to the side of the road. "Oh man …" He kicked open his door and popped open the hood. The engine sizzled, more acrid vapor filling the air.

I hopped out of the truck and stood by Sam, placing my hands on my hips. "Well, that's a fine mess."

Sam looked at me miserably. "I'm sorry. I'll just have to …" He trailed off and rubbed the back of his neck.

A groan escaped my mouth. "We'll just have to walk to the nearest house and telephone Beatrice. Naturally."

I began walking down the dirt road, the warm sun on my back. Sam trailed along beside me, muttering to himself. "Don't worry about the truck," I said, smiling. "It's a nice day for a walk anyway."

"I know, I know. I just feel …" Sam kicked at a rock. "Silly, I guess."

"Don't feel silly." I straightened. "You drove me all the way out here in the middle of nowhere to get paint for my shed and baking soda for my … for Beatrice."

Sam grinned. "The baking soda was in town."

"That doesn't matter." The sun was beginning to feel warm, so I pulled off my sweater and let it hang on my arm. "How far until the nearest house, you think?"

A look of concentration passed over Sam's face. "I think we passed one five minutes ago in the truck."

"That could be twenty minutes on foot."

"True."

Oh well. I sighed and let my fingers run through the tall grass on my side. "Don't you think it's pretty out here?"

Sam looked around and seemed to consider this. "Yes," he decided. "It's peaceful, at least. Beautiful and calm."

I nodded. "I want to live in the country someday. Far away from the world ... in my own little haven of beauty."

Sam licked his lips. "That would be nice. But I'm starting to grow fond of the seashore." He glanced sideways at me.

Just look straight ahead. "Well, then, we'll have to visit each other. Just to get a break from our own paradises and enjoy someone else's."

Sam nodded.

"I can't wait to meet your wife one day." I risked a peek and studied Sam's profile.

He glanced at me out of the side of his eye. "What are you thinking?" he asked softly.

"I'm just trying to imagine what kind of person you would marry. Someone happy, I think. Someone who would make you laugh and smile all the time. A girl with a happy, cheerful disposition." I nudged him playfully.

Sam avoided my eye and looked at the ground. "Well, don't think about it too much. You'll hurt your head." He straightened his shoulders. "Besides, I already have a girl I mean to marry."

I bit my lip. My stomach felt like it had dropped—I hadn't even realized it was floating.

"Oh, really? Is she from Tennessee?" I hadn't seen him around any girls here, had I? *Not besides Charlie, and she doesn't count.*

"Yeah." Sam fell silent.

"Oh." I brightened my voice. "Well, tell me about her." *I hate her.* Panic gripped my stomach. *Wait, how can I hate her when I haven't met her?* My head felt dizzy.

Sam's voice, in turn, became tight. "You'll meet her some-day." He halted, causing me to ram into his back. "Oh, here's the house."

We rang the doorbell and asked to use the telephone. I called Beatrice and explained the situation, promising to meet her by the truck. We hung up and headed back, walking too fast to talk. At least that's what I told myself.

Beatrice pulled up just as we were swinging into the bed of the truck. She leaned out the car window and smiled. "Nice truck you have there, Sam Carroll."

Sam reddened. "Thanks."

"Don't worry, I called a car mechanic. He should be on his way."

We hauled the cans of paint, thinner, and the baking soda into the car and waited for the mechanic. I leaned against the truck and smiled. "Thanks for taking me driving."

Sam grinned back, squinting from the sun. "'Twas a plea-sure, my lady."

Chapter 13

The Heart has narrow Banks
It measures like the Sea
In mighty—unremitting Bass
And Blue Monotony.

—Emily Dickinson

I lay awake in bed and took in the sounds of Beatrice walking about downstairs. *She should have left for church by now.*

I listened for the signal—the sound of the front door clicking shut. As soon as I heard it, I leaped out of bed and ran to the window. Sure enough, Beatrice's car was pulling out of the driveway.

With a victorious sigh, I walked over to the dresser and opened up the top drawer, locating my notebook and grabbing a pen. Moments later I was through the screen door, the sunny, blue sky greeting me to a perfect day.

My light-blue skirt fluttered in the wind as I sat on the sandy oceanfront, my notebook perched on my lap. I traced my finger across the words, a faint smile on my face. My finger meandered to the opposite page, where I had drawn a charcoal print of the starry night sky. A sky I remember gazing on by the lake as my mother proclaimed me a star as well.

I bent my head and watched the water coming in around me, making my skirts swirl in the sand. On a whim I stood and placed my notebook on a rock, safely away from the sea.

The sand tickled my bare feet as I waded into the warm water, and my dress clung to my legs as the waves hit my body. Once I reached my knees, I sunk down, submerging my head under water, only to come up spitting out salty water and sand. I coughed and shook my soaking-wet head. *Well, that was dumb.*

But I was already in the ocean, and I might as well enjoy it. I ran my fingers through the water, making little rippling waves. My skirts billowed out around me like the petals of a giant flower. I laughed and pushed them down under the water.

The floating skirts gave me an idea. With some trepidation, I leaned backward until I was floating on the surface of the water. I closed my eyes and breathed in the salty, intoxicating air.

So this is what bliss feels like ... I smiled. *Sweet paradise.*

"Allie!" someone shouted.

I screamed and flailed. My feet failed to find ground, and I disappeared under the water, kicking and shrieking as salt water filled my lungs.

A rough hand grabbed my arm and jerked me above the surface, dragging me to the shore just when I was sure I was going to die. I crawled onto the dry sand and lay heaving on my stomach. I coughed up water and sand and who knows what else, gasping for breath.

Sam Carroll was shaking his wet head at me. "Gosh, you're so stupid sometimes, Allie. You know you can't swim very well." He ran a hand over his face and frowned. "What were you thinking?"

I narrowed my eyes at him and turned around to sit on my sandy bottom. "I was perfectly fine until you came along and made me *drown*."

"You would have drowned for real if I hadn't saved you." Sam glared at me. I glared back.

I lifted my chin and reached down to wring out my wet, now filthy dress. "I was floating."

Sam cocked an eyebrow and dusted off his pants.

Avoiding his glance, I scrambled up off the ground and headed toward the rocks. "Why aren't you in church, anyway?"

"Why aren't *you* at church? I assumed Beatrice made you go." Sam followed me.

I gave him a withering glance as I picked up my journal and wiped it off. "She and I have an agreement. I'm not religious."

"Yeah, I remember." Sam stuck his hands in his pockets and watched me. "Why is that?"

The question caught me off guard. I froze, crouched near the ground, and pulled my journal tight against my stomach. "I'm just not. Mama hated Christianity, and she told me I should as well."

"Well, that seems ridiculous." A teasing glint caught in Sam's eye, balanced out by something bordering on serious. He ran a hand through his hair until it stood up a little. "I never took you as the type to do what someone else wanted you to."

I stuck up my nose and climbed to my feet. "This coming from the son of a Sunday school teacher?"

"My parents aren't the reason I'm a Christian. Their faith has nothing to do with mine."

"I thought your mother——"

Sam kicked a stone, sending it yards out of sight. "Please don't mention my mother."

I started walking toward the house. Sam slowed down a bit and fell behind me. When I looked over my shoulder, I saw him grimace. "Sam, what's the——" I gasped. "Oh, my goodness! What happened to your foot?"

Sam looked down at his foot and shrugged. "I must have cut it on a shell."

He had a large gash on his left heel and blood trickled into the sand.

"Sam Carroll, how could you walk around in the dirt with your foot like that? You're going to end up dying of an infection!" I gaped at him.

Sam avoided my eye. "I was headed home. It's only a couple hundred yards away."

"How could you say that? You'll never make it up the hill on that bad foot, and I can't carry you!" I ran a hand through my sand-matted hair and rolled my eyes. "Just come into the house and I'll clean it up."

* * * * *

Sam followed me into the kitchen.

"Up on the counter," I commanded. *Where did Beatrice move the medicine?* I rummaged through the cabinets until I found a bottle of salve. "Here we go."

I lifted his foot and gently washed off the blood and sand.

Little cuts pierced the rough skin, with bits of shell stuck in the sores. Sam winced and gripped the counter, making my stomach squeeze even more. "This'll help." I smoothed the ointment onto the cut and ignored Sam's groan.

Almost done ... I reached beneath the sink and pulled out a clean rag, ripping it into shreds and wrapped Sam's foot.

"There." I patted the foot and looked up.

Sam was smiling. "Once again, I thank you for tending my wounds."

I screwed the top back on the salve. "What are you talking about?"

Sam looked at me quizzically. "Don't you remember?" He held up his hand, where a small scar crossed his palm.

I sucked in a quick breath and shook my head, gathering up the supplies. "Apparently not," I lied. My hands quivered as I carried the medical tools back to the cabinet. *Don't let him make you feel this way, Allie. Don't listen to a word he says.*

"Oh." Sam sounded deflated. "Well, I cut my hands helping you in the garden and you bandaged them up for me."

I peeked over my shoulder. He was smiling to himself as he turned over his hands.

"I told you I thought you were pretty, and you told me to go home." Sam chuckled. "I still think you're pretty, Allie." His voice softened. "Beautiful, in fact. Even with sand and grime in your hair. And I think you're smart and funny and sweet and ... *perfect.*"

I placed a hand on my hip, suddenly feeling sick of it all. "What is your problem, Sam? What are you doing here?"

He shrugged. "Well, I saw you from my window and ..."

I raised a hand, cutting him off. My mind was racing. "No. It's not just that." I took a step back and looked him over, frowning. "Why are you always here? You've always just sort of *been here.* There is no reason whatsoever that you should be here on this beach on Sunday morning at the *exact* same time as me." My eyes became slits. "There isn't even a reason why you should be in Maine, living three houses down from me and popping back into my life."

Sam bit his lip, running a hand through his hair. "I can explain."

"So do it." I crossed my arms. "Explain."

Sam looked at his foot. "I didn't want you to find out, because I didn't want you to get mad at me."

"About what?" I rolled my eyes. "You are making no sense at all."

"Remember that time I went out of town for three weeks to visit Aunt Rachel in Maine?" He frowned. "It was right before your mother died."

I shrugged. "Yeah, what about it?"Sam took a deep breath. "Well, I told Aunt Rachel about your mother. And how she was sick and dying ..." He scrunched his face. "I was worried about you, Allie. So when I found out about Beatrice and how she was lonely and wanted another daughter ..." He trailed off, staring at the ground. "I just thought you would be happy with her."

The floor seemed to shift beneath me as I took another step back. *I don't believe this. I don't believe this.* "Wait." I pointed a finger at Sam. "*You* arranged for Beatrice to adopt me?"

He licked his lips. "No, actually Beatrice arranged it, once Aunt Rachel told her about you. She has a really big heart, Allie." His eyes pleaded with me to understand.

I shook my head. My eyes began to sting. I rubbed them and turned away. "You had no right." My voice shook. "No right at all to interfere with my life and my future."

"Allie, I was young. And I worried about you. I just wanted you to be happy."

I spun around, shooting every ounce of anger I possessed at his body. "What made you think you had permission to come into my life and ruin it?"

Sam shook his head desperately. "I wasn't thinking, Allie. I loved you."

My stomach twisted in knots. I gripped my skirt and tried to swallow the hot tears in my throat.

Sam's voice began to rise. "I still love you, Allie. I love you so much that I stayed away from Maine for four years. I knew you were grieving and I didn't want to pop up and … ruin your life. So I waited. I was hoping I'd forget you." He looked down. "I knew you'd forgotten me. And then I came here. Once I saw you …" He trailed off, waving a hand. "I knew I hadn't forgotten you at all. And I knew you'd be angry, so I didn't tell you what I'd done. Which was selfish and stupid and just goes to prove what a jerk I am." He jumped off the counter and looked down at me. I hoped he stepped right on the cut.

My mind was racing. I backed away from him, bumping my head against one of Beatrice's cabinets.

"But I never meant to hurt you." He lowered his voice. "I just wanted to be with you. I've always wanted to be with you, to see you and make you as happy as you make me." He reached out and touched my hair, smiling softly.

It was my turn to speak, but when I opened my mouth no

185

words came out. My wrist throbbed; I looked down and saw my white knuckles gripping the countertop. I let go and stuck them behind my back, avoiding Sam's eyes. "Go home, Sam," I whispered.

There was a pause. And then, "Allie, I don't understand."

I opened the cabinet and placed the salve inside, closing the door with a slam. I turned around. "I'm sorry. But you have to go home."

Sam ran a hand through his wet hair. "Don't you see, Allie? You're the girl I mean to marry. You're the girl I'm crazy about."

I gripped my skirt, water from the ocean still running down my legs. "I'm sorry, but I can't do that."

"Why not?"

The lump in my throat threatened to choke me and my eyes were burning. "Because I don't love you." I bit my lip until I could feel blood on my tongue.

"But I thought …" Sam looked bewildered, and continued to run his hand through his wet hair, as if he couldn't stop. He straightened. "Is this about Aunt Rachel? Or my mother? Because we never have to see them again. I just want to—"

I sucked the inside of my cheek and stared out the window. "It's just not meant to be, Sam. Just go before you make it worse." My words sounded cold and flat. I slid my eyes shut. *I can't believe this is happening.*

Sam hobbled toward me. He grabbed my shoulders and spun me so that I had no choice but to face him. He shook his head, his blue eyes filled with disbelief.

"Allie, you've got to be kidding me." He squeezed my shoulders. "Don't you see we're perfect for each other? We're alike, you and me. We think and act the same. We're both stubborn and proud and difficult ... but that's what makes us right for each other." He searched my eyes desperately.

I lifted my chin. "Good-bye, Sam."

He looked me up and down, disgusted, and stuffed his hands into his pockets. "Good-bye, Allie." Plates rattled as he stormed out of the kitchen, the screen door slamming behind him.

I rushed to the window and watched him stomp down the beach, slowing down to a defeated limp.

I closed the curtains and sat alone in the dark kitchen, tears coursing down my cheeks. *Why should I care whether he stays or goes? He had no business stepping into my life. No business at all.*

I sighed and hugged my chest, sliding down against the cabinets. My body collapsed into itself as soon as I hit the floor.

Why should I care what anyone thinks of me?

* * * * *

"Soda?"

I jerked my head up. Irene was smiling at me from behind the counter, a Coke bottle in her hand.

"Thanks," I muttered. I popped the lid off and ran my finger around the cold rim.

The diner was empty, the wistful sound of Bing Crosby floating from the jukebox. "You should have that thing painted pink."

Irene glanced at it and wrinkled her nose. "I don't think I've *ever* seen a pink jukebox, honey. But I suppose I could have the first." She hummed to herself as she stacked clean dishes on the shelf behind the counter. "As soon as Daniel comes home, we'll paint it pink and throw a party, with the happiest music you could think of. He's just got to finish his overseas duty first. Then we'll have a great time."

I wish. I slumped my arms on the counter and stared at the ticking clock. *How could I go from feeling happy one week to completely miserable the next? Darn that Samuel Carroll for coming to Maine and making my life awful.*

Irene reached out a hand and rested it on my arm. Her long pink fingernails massaged little circles on my skin. "What's wrong?" she asked. "You seem a little out of it."

I pushed the Coke away and buried my face in my hands. "Sam ruined our friendship."

Irene's breathing picked up. "Did he say something ugly to you? Should I be *infuriated* with him?"

"No." I shook my head. "It's just …" I couldn't tell Irene what he'd done about Beatrice. I crossed and uncrossed my legs. "Last week he told me that he loves me. I haven't talked to him since."

I looked up at Irene. Realization dawned in her green eyes. "Oh … I see." She made her way around the counter and pulled out a bar chair, sliding in next to me. "And you don't love him back."

"Of course not!" *He's Sam Carroll, for goodness' sake.*

Irene bit her lip and grunted. "And did you know that he loved you?"

My heart sank. I flashed back to all the times he'd followed me when I was little … to all the times he'd gone out of his way to make me laugh … to all the times I'd caught him staring at me.

"Yes," I muttered.

"I see." Irene smiled. "Well, you know, Mom *always says* —"

Suddenly the diner door swung open and two young men strolled in. My stomach lurched at the sight. Sam and Russell.

Irene brightened and stepped behind the counter. "Good afternoon, gentlemen. What will it be?"

Russell slid into a seat beside me. "Hi, Allie." He looked around. "Um … is Charlie here?"

I shook my head and glanced at Sam. He was ignoring me, frowning hard at the menu. My cheeks grew hot.

"I'll just have a root beer float," Russell said, turning back to Irene.

"Coming right up!" Irene glanced at me. "Oh, Allie, can you change the song on the jukebox? I think number thirty-eight would be *quite* fitting." She gave a little wink.

I slid out of my seat and walked over to the jukebox. *Number thirty-eight* … Benny Goodman's orchestra filled the air. "Taking a Chance on Love." I made a face. *Seriously, Irene?*

Sam was fiddling with a straw when I got back to the bar. He glanced at me and reddened.

This is just great. I can't even sit in the same room as him. I glared at the jukebox. *Especially with this stupid song playing.*

"I'm just gonna go," I mumbled, pushing away from the bar. I reached into my pocket but Irene waved me away.

"It's free." She lowered her voice and leaned her head toward me. "And Allie," she whispered, "don't be afraid of yourself. Just a thought." She shot her eyes to Sam and turned back to the soda fountain.

I shuffled out of the diner, my eyes glued to the floor. *I feel like a five-year-old.* I could only imagine what Russell and Sam were thinking. *Why is life so complicated?*

* * * * *

Beatrice frowned and motioned at my plate with her fork. "Aren't you hungry?"

I looked at the potatoes turning into cold lumps before me. "Not really."

Beatrice's face pinched in concern. "What's wrong?"

"It's just ..." I sighed and pushed around the food on my plate. "I had a fight with Sam and now he won't speak to me."

"What did you two fight about?"

"Nothing." I went back to pushing around my food. *Why did I think she would understand?*

"Allie," Beatrice lowered her voice. "You know you can talk to me."

I looked up into her dark-brown eyes, hidden behind wire glasses. "I don't think I'm what he expected me to be."

"What do you mean?"

Tears stung at my eyes. "I'm mean and rude and he's obviously prideful, and I just ... I just don't think we fit well together."

Beatrice tapped her chin with her finger. "Have you tried apologizing?"

"No." *I don't apologize. Ever.* I looked down.

"Sam seems like a nice boy. I'd hate to see you stay mad at him for no apparent reason." Beatrice nodded at my food. "You'd better eat, though. It wouldn't serve you any better to be upset *and* hungry."

I gave her a small smile and took a bite of potatoes.

The doorbell rang. I pushed back my chair and dropped my napkin. "I'll see who that is."

"Don't tarry too long. Your supper will get cold!" Beatrice called.

I laughed. "It already is!"

I swung open the front door and came to an immediate stop. Sam Carroll stood in front of me, swaying back and forth. "Um … can I talk to you?"

I nodded and stepped out onto the porch, shutting the door behind me and leaning against the house for support. My heart was pounding in my chest.

"I, uh …" Sam took off his hat and ran his fingers through his hair. "I came to say I was sorry. I acted rude and childish and you don't deserve that."

He was staring at me with his blue eyes, looking so honest and sorry. "How do you know what I deserve?" I whispered.

Sam gave me a crooked smile. "Wanna go for a walk?"

I nodded and followed him down the steps, ignoring the screaming pain of hot rocks beneath my bare feet. Finally we reached the sand. I looked up and saw Sam staring at me.

"You must be really mad at me," he said.

I shook my head. "I was at that moment, but——"

"I deserve it," Sam interrupted.

"No, you don't." I frowned. "You should be the one mad at me. I spoke very cruelly to you. I'm sorry."

"It's okay. You can't help it if you don't love me, can you?" Sam gave me a wry smile.

My stomach pinched. "I, uh … I guess we can be friends again now."

Sam looked as if the thought had never occurred to him. "Of course. I hope we're always friends."

"Me too," I whispered. And I meant it. I knelt and picked up a shell, letting the sand trickle out. "I love seashells."

Sam grinned. "They're very pretty—as long as I have shoes on."

"Well, this is a good shell." I tucked the shell in my pocket. "Save it for a rainy day," I explained. "Something Mama taught me."

Sam wrung his hands, looking nervous. "I, um … I telephoned my mother today."

"Oh?"

"Yeah." He stopped and squinted at the sun sinking into the ocean. Soft shades of pink and orange flickered over his face. "I told her that from now on I'm making my own decisions, but that I still want her to support me. I still need her to support me."

"That's wonderful." I felt a pang in my chest. "I'm happy for you." I turned and started walking back up the beach, fighting the impulse to grab his hand and squeeze it. *That would be a dumb thing to do.* I nibbled my lip. "Are you going back home?"

"No."

"Oh." I felt pressure release in my chest. "Good." I couldn't help the silly smile that spread across my face.

Sam stopped in front of my door and bowed charmingly. "Good night, m'lady."

I fought back giggles. "Good night."

I stood in the doorway and watched him trudge back toward his aunt's house, whistling to himself. Then I shut the door and leaned against it, closing my eyes.

"Who was that?" My lids flashed open. Beatrice stood by the staircase, holding my dinner plate in her hand.

"Sam." I began walking up the stairs. My cheeks hurt from smiling. I felt light and bubbly, like I needed to spread my sunshine. I scurried back down and leaned over, planting a quick kiss on Beatrice's cheek. "Good night."

Beatrice's eyes widened. "Good night."

I ran up the stairs and into my room. Opening my journal, I grabbed a roll of masking tape and fastened the seashell to an empty page. I smiled and stroked the smooth shell. *For a rainy day.*

* * * * *

"Russell is perfect for me," Charlie sighed, leaning back into the vinyl seat. "We have so much in common with each other."

"Like *what*?" The sarcasm in my voice stung. I winced and looked down.

Charlie grimaced. "Well, we both enjoy things like riding bikes and looking at the stars."

"Oh." I fingered the rim of my milkshake glass and looked around the nearly empty diner. *But their characters aren't similar— their strengths and weaknesses aren't the same like ...* I shook my head to clear my thoughts and downed my shake.

Charlie smiled. "Russell's going to grow up to be a famous scientist, Allie. I just know it! And once he gets back from the war—"

I jerked up in my seat. "Russell's going to war?"

Charlie's big blue eyes watered up. "Yes. Russell's leaving the first week of June, before he gets drafted ... Sam's going too, I think. He departs next week. Though I'm sure you know that already — you see each other so often now." She twisted the ring on her finger. I hadn't even noticed she was wearing it.

"But Russell says before he leaves" — Charlie's voice quivered with excitement — "he'll marry me and I'll be Mrs. Russell Wilkinson. Oh, Allie, he asked me last night!"

Charlie began going on about the proposal and waved her ring at me, but my mind was rushing. *Sam was going to the war? Why didn't he tell me?* My blood started to boil. *What's wrong with him? He could at least have had the decency to ...*

By the time I refocused, Charlie was sighing and gazing off in the distance, rambling on about Russell's virtues. "He's so kind and gentle, and when he smiles at me ...." She glanced at me as if realizing something for the first time. "You know, I always thought I wanted to marry Russell in order to be rich and happy. But now I want to marry him because I honestly think I would make him happy too." She gripped my arm. "Allie, I've never felt this way about any boy before. I think he's the first ever man I've really fallen in love with."

Sam's going to war. I pushed my milkshake away and bolted out of my seat. I thought I heard Charlie shouting after me once I burst through the swinging door, but I was to the car before she had a chance to catch up.

My hand gripped the steering wheel unsteadily as my thoughts whirled. Someone honked at me as I raced past the grocery store.

What is Sam thinking? He can't go to Europe!

I pushed my free hand through my hair. If he kept acting up like this I would die of a heart attack before I was thirty.

Blood pounded in my ears as I pulled into the driveway. As I opened the car door, I saw another car whiz down the road, with Sam behind the wheel.

"Sam!" I slammed shut the door and tried to run down the street. My foot twisted in my heels. "Dratted things," I muttered as I pulled off my shoes.

Sam's car slowed to a stop, allowing me to arrive at the window just as Sam stuck his head out.

"Sam Carroll, what in the world are you thinking? You're so ... *obtuse* sometimes!" I screamed, waving one of my shoes at him.

He cocked an eyebrow. "Is that an insult? I'm sorry, but I don't speak the higher language."

I leaned forward and shoved him. He moved back in his seat, shielding himself. "Hey, what was that for?"

"For joining the army!" I shoved him again. *Why do I have to know him? Why do I have to put up with him?*

"Why shouldn't I join the army? It's always been my dream and you know it." Sam was bristling now. "You said yourself that if it wasn't for the men who gave their lives on the battlefield, we wouldn't have the same freedoms we do today."

"Because you could get killed!" I screamed.

"Why should you care if I get killed?" Sam's voice was rising too. His blue eyes were set in challenge.

"If you die, I'll be all alone!" Honestly, how could he be so *idiotic*? My chest rose and fell as I stared at him.

"Why do you care if you're all alone?"

"Because I love you!" I hit him as hard as I could with my high heel. His eyes widened.

My eyes widened too, and I turned around and ran, dropping my shoes on the ground.

"Allie!" I heard Sam's shoes on the gravel behind me, hopping out of the car. I closed my eyes and ran down the street, past my house, and toward the beach. My bare feet blistered on the hot sand, forcing me to slow down when I reached the waterfront. I bit my lip and stared at the ocean, refusing to turn around.

"Allie?" Sam stopped somewhere behind me. I listened to him panting.

I wiggled my toes in the cool water.

"Allie, I love you." Sam cleared his throat, which had started to sound clogged. "I know I have to go away, but I don't want to go without knowing for sure that you love me too. Allie, I want you to marry me." His voice cracked and stopped.

My heart felt wrenched. I balled up my toes in the sand and took a deep breath. "How do I know you won't leave me too?" I bit my lip. "How do I know for sure that you'll be okay?"

"Allie …" Sam sighed and touched my shoulder, turning me to face him. I wiped my cheeks before I looked him in the eyes. "Allie," he said gently, "I can't promise you that I'll be here forever, or even for long, but I can promise I will love you for as long as I'm alive."

I looked at my feet, but Sam reached up a finger to lift my chin. "Allie?" he whispered, stroking my cheek. His eyes looked so scared—so worried that I would reject him and shove him out for good.

I took a deep breath and gave him a shaky smile. "I love you, Sam Carroll."

He smiled too and pulled me close, reaching out to hold my hand.

"Allie!" a voice shouted.

I jumped back to see Beatrice standing on the porch, scanning the yard for us. "I'm right here, Beatrice!" I shouted, waving my hand.

"Oh, there you are!" Beatrice smiled at us. "Sam, there's a police officer here saying something about a car parked in the middle of the road!"

Sam gave me a crazy grin and called back, "I'll be right there!"

Beatrice nodded and turned back inside.

Sam rolled his eyes and grabbed my hand, running back to the house. "Come on. It appears the constable doesn't understand love."

* * * * *

I pulled up my knees to my chest and sighed. In front of me was a blank journal page. As the words played in my head, my chest felt so tight I thought it would burst. I leaned my head against the windowsill and closed my eyes, savoring the moment.

Then I opened them and picked up my pen.

August 19, 1943

Mama,

I stared at the word. All alone on the page, it suddenly seemed the loneliest four letters in existence.

I couldn't remember the last time I had written Mama.

Maybe sometime at the beginning of the summer? Before Sam came? Before everything turned upside down and crazy.

Mama ... I pressed the pen to my lips. It was cool and smooth, chilling my mouth.

Mama,

I think I am engaged. To Sam. You remember him, right? I imagine you approve of him, because you always seemed to take a liking to him, even when I didn't. I love him. I really do. But I don't want to see him go. It hurts to love someone and lose them. I don't know what I would do if that happened again.

I want to hold this love inside of me, because I'm afraid if I let it out, he'll take it with him and I'll lose him. Then I won't be able to get the love back, and there'll be a hole in my heart where it used to be. I have my love for you, and my love for Sam. But if I lose him too, I won't have any love left over. And then I'll just feel empty—like you did with Dad. I think that is my biggest fear.

* * * * *

"You look lovely, Allie," Sam whispered, kissing my gloved hand.

My heart squeezed. I tilted down my hat so that no one would see the tear sliding down my cheek. "Thank you." I managed a smile. "You don't look so bad yourself." I fixed a crease in his uniform.

Sam lifted my chin and wiped away the tear. "Don't cry."

I looked away. It was too much to see Sam in his newly pressed uniform standing in front of me. Especially with a young couple embracing on the other side of the station; the girl was weeping as her sweetheart kissed her.

"Allie," Sam whispered. "I'll be back."

"I know." I gulped and focused on a spot near his shoulder.

"And then we'll hear the church bells ring and you'll look beautiful in that white dress." Sam squeezed my hand, his voice growing shaky.

"I'd like to have a June wedding, so I can have roses," I whispered, looking up at him. "My mother loved roses."

Sam nodded. "I remember." A whistle shrilled and smoke filled the station. I coughed as my lungs began to cloud up. I gripped Sam's sleeves and looked up to see the train rolling onto the platform.

"Sam?"

"Yes, Allie?"

I looked down and brushed off his uniform, taking a deep breath. I raised my chin. "Just be careful."

Sam cleared his throat. "If I write to you, will you write to me?"

I fought down the hot, sick feeling in my stomach and managed to nod. "Of course," I said, a bit more sharply than I intended. "If I find time."

Sam just smiled at me. "I'll pass the time by imagining you—reading Emily Dickinson and writing in that little notebook of yours." He chuckled. "I hope you don't glare at any other young men while I'm gone."

"I'll try to resist," I said sarcastically.

"All aboard!" A man yelled, hopping off the train.

Sam gave my hand one last squeeze and leaned in to kiss me on the cheek. "Good-bye, Allie," he whispered. "I love you."

"I love you," I whispered back.

And then it was all over, and in a puff of smoke the train was pulling away from me. I realized I was alone and frantically looked for Sam. There he was, sticking his head out of a window and giving me a little wave.

I pressed my gloved hand to my cheek. It suddenly felt cold.

* * * * *

"Allie?" Beatrice called as I walked into the kitchen and dropped the keys on the table. I sank into a chair and stared out the window.

Beatrice came in from the living room and glanced at me. I ignored her and continued to watch a caterpillar inch its way up the glass.

From the parlor, a Billie Holiday record was playing. "I'll be seeing you," her voice crooned, "in all the old familiar places ..."

"Could you turn that off?" I asked sharply.

A few seconds later, the room was silent. Beatrice poked her head in the doorway of the kitchen, holding a half-finished sock. "Are you okay, Allie?"

I reached up to wipe a tear off my cheek before smoothing back my hair. "Of course. I'm fine. I just have a headache."

Beatrice pulled out a chair and sat down, her eyes on her knitting. "Did things not go well at the station?"

I shook my head. "They went as well as they could go."

Beatrice reached out and squeezed my knee. "He'll come home soon. In the blink of an eye, in fact." She snapped a finger. "And then we'll have a big wedding right here at the house!"

She fidgeted with her needles and glanced up. "Still unhappy?" she asked in a low voice. "Do you want to talk about it?"

I bit the inside of my cheek. How typical of Beatrice—to be utterly concerned with my life and my friends, wanting to help me piece my heart back together, when it was clear there was nothing she could do.

My stomach churned. "Never mind," I muttered.

I ran to my bedroom and sank to the floor against the door, burying my head in my knees. I felt sick, like when I was little and Mama used to hold back my hair while I threw up.

I sniffled. *Oh, Mama, why couldn't you be here now?*

Chapter 14

Sometimes with the Heart
Seldom with the Soul
Scarcer once with the Might
Few — love at all.

—Emily Dickinson

"It was a *beautiful* wedding," Irene remarked, sipping her pink lemonade beside me on the porch. She watched me out of the corner of her eye.

I nodded, fingering the wood grains on the old rocking chair. The white paint was chipped and peeling, and I tore several flakes away.

"Charlie was a lovely bride." I smiled. "She was just glowing."

"Russell certainly seemed happy enough." Irene laughed. "I thought his shaky knees would give way and he would *collapse* at the altar."

"Would have been interesting." I took a long sip of my tea and sighed. "Wouldn't say I'd want it to happen, but—" I stopped abruptly and ran my finger along the rim of the glass. *If only ...*

"Do you miss him?" Irene asked, reading my thoughts.

I shrugged. "He writes." I bit my lip and fought the burning sensation behind my eyelids. "The last letter contained a dried rose. He knows I wanted a June wedding." I squinted up at the sky and sighed. "Maybe next year."

"Do you write back?" Irene probed, watching me.

I avoided her glance. "Every now and then."

Irene sighed and put down her glass. "What are you afraid of, Allie?" She paused, raising a red eyebrow. "Of getting too attached?"

I sucked in a gasp of air. *I don't want to lose him.* Several more paint flakes tore under my fingers. "I just want to be certain that, if the worst should happen, I'll be ready."

"Allie, you block out everyone. Even yourself." She shook her head. "I noticed it when you came here and I figured I'd just ignore it. I thought that over time you would open up and allow us to love you, and love us back. But you haven't. You've just held on to this bitterness inside of you and let it grow into this huge ..." She held up a hand. "I don't even know what to call it. Can't you see this ... *shell* you've built around yourself? You block out everyone. Even yourself."

"I do not have a shell!" I bristled.

"See there!" Irene pointed, her eyes widening. "You're defensive to a *fault*. Every time someone tries to show they care about you, you take it as an insult. Why don't you ever let your guard down and relax?"

I put down my tea and began to stand. "I have things to do, Irene. I need to ..."

She rolled her eyes and reached out to stop me. "Just sit for a second, Allie."

I sat back down, rigid. *Here we go . . .*

"I want to talk to you about Mom," Irene said. "Have you noticed anything strange about her lately?"

"About Beatrice?" I shrugged. "I don't pay attention to her much."

Irene shrugged. "It's probably nothing. She's just been complaining of headaches. Maybe I should take her to the doctor."

"Ha. Doctors can't do a thing." *Look where they got Mama.* I stood and headed inside.

"Allie?"

I looked over my shoulder to see Irene smiling timidly at me. She tucked a piece of hair behind her ear. "I'm sorry if I hurt your feelings," she said softly. "I just care about you, that's all." She looked up at me with her big green eyes, looking sad. "I want you to be happy."

I paused in the doorway, my heart caught somewhere between the inside and the outside. *My happiness died four years ago.*

I nodded at Irene and went inside, the screen door slamming behind me.

* * * * *

I folded the last of the clothes and began stacking them in the basket. My hand smoothed over a plaid dress as my mind wandered.

When was the last time I wrote to Sam? I frowned, trying to remember. *Probably a few weeks ago.*

Maybe Irene was right. Maybe I should write him.

I headed up the stairs, laundry basket in hand. What would I say? My life was so boring. And he always wrote the most interesting things — talking about Europe, and tanks, and his daily life.

I paused on the step. No, actually, he never wrote about his doings. Only what he wished he was doing.

Which was usually being close to me.

I leaned against the wall and closed my eyes, trying to imagine life on the warfront. I pictured Sam, ragged and worn, with mud smeared across his face and uniform. He carried a large gun in his rough hands and had a heavy sack thrown over his back. I could just see him lifting the gun to his eye and aiming at a German boy, shells exploding behind him.

A shudder ran through my body. *What would I ever do if …*

I pushed the thought out of my mind and walked down the hallway to Beatrice's room. I slowed in the doorway and raised my hand to knock.

"And please be with my Irene, and bless her and give her the strength she needs to go on without Daniel here beside her."

I paused and peeked into the room. Beatrice was kneeling by the bed, her gray hair hanging down her back. Her head was bent in prayer.

"Lord, I know how it feels to have to face each day without a husband beside you. But I pray that Daniel will continue to stay safe and will come back to us soon. And may Irene continue to trust in you, knowing that you will comfort her and stay close by her forever. Lord, I love her and only want what's best for her. You know that."

My heart squeezed. Of course she loved Irene. Irene was her daughter — her flesh and blood.

I knelt to place Beatrice's clothes on the floor and turned to leave.

"And, Lord, please be with Allie."

I froze, afraid to turn for fear she'd hear me. Pressing my cheek to the wall, I bent my ear toward the open door.

"Lord," Beatrice's voice drew strained. She coughed several times before continuing. "Lord, I just don't know how to comfort her. I can't imagine what that child's been through to harden her heart like that. I've prayed for years, and she still shuts out anything I offer. Lord, continue to give me the daily strength I need to show Allie that I love her and care about her. Help me to reach through all the barriers she has set up around herself and let her know I don't want to replace her mother; I just want to love her. And Lord—" Beatrice's voice began to break. "Lord, please soften her heart toward you. Please let her experience your love and come to drink of your salvation. Please melt her heart of stone and please give her a heart of flesh. Let her learn to truly love, and to accept being loved. I know you can reach her even when I cannot. I ask these things in your precious name ... Amen."

I moved from the doorway and rushed into my room, quietly shutting the door behind me.

What was that all about? Beatrice prays for me?

My heart felt a strange flutter. I tried to remember what Mama had said about religion. She had called it superstitious nonsense.

Was Beatrice a superstitious fool? She certainly hadn't seemed so.

Christians will make you feel loved — make you feel wanted. Mama's words rang in my ears. *But they don't mean any of it.*

I began unbuttoning my dress, pausing when I caught a glance of myself in the mirror. My mother's face looked back at me. I was like her in so many ways.

But Mama had loved. She loved me, at least.

I went back to undressing. Had Beatrice really meant those things she said? She couldn't have been trying to trick me. She didn't even know I was there.

Her words played over and over again in my mind. Was there a God who wanted me to … Well, what did he want me to do?

I crossed over to my bed and opened up my journal. Smoothing out the paper, I raised my pen to the paper.

May 27, 1944

I stared at the empty page. For once, I had nothing to say.

What am I thinking? I don't need a God. I can depend on myself for anything I need.

My hand was still on the blank page. I stared at it. In my mind's eye, I could see Charlie shrugging, looking doubtful. *What if it's not enough?*

I closed the journal and turned out the light. Beatrice's words played over in my head. "Melt her heart of stone …"

The room had never seemed so dark and quiet before. I rolled on my side and curled my fist. What if my heart *couldn't* melt?

Chapter 15

Far from love the Heavenly Father
Leads the chosen child;
Oftener through realm of briar
Than the meadow mild.

—Emily Dickinson

I lay in bed and listened to Beatrice walking about downstairs. She was probably going to leave for church any time.

I wonder what she does there.

I hadn't been in years—not since my mother's funeral. I stared at the cracks on the ceiling. *Maybe I'll go ... just this once.*

I would never have to go again. But it wouldn't hurt to go just once—to see what it was like.

I climbed out of bed, brushed my teeth, and pulled my best blue dress out of the closet. I slipped it over my head and sat down at the mirror to examine myself.

My dark brown hair fell down my back in soft waves. I brushed them out and pinned them up on my neck. If I brushed just a tiny bit of powder on my nose, you couldn't see those faded little freckles.

I pinned a hat on my head and sat back to check myself. *Don't I look silly — all dressed up on a Sunday morning.* I scrunched my nose out of habit.

My shoulders slumped as I stared at myself. *I do look ridiculous. Everyone will stare at me when I get there.* I bit my lip. *They'll know I don't belong.*

"Allie!" Beatrice shouted from downstairs. "I'm leaving! I'll be back around noon!"

"Wait!" I jumped up and ran to grab my shoes. "I'm coming with you!"

I bounded down the hall and skidded to a halt in the stairwell. Beatrice was waiting at the bottom of the steps, disbelief etched on her face. She clutched the railing and looked me over. I straightened my back and brushed past her, heading for the car.

Beatrice slid into the driver's seat quietly. She turned on the ignition and gripped the steering wheel, and we rolled down the street in silence.

It was a beautiful Sunday morning. May was in full bloom — roses and wild blueberries were budding everywhere.

I squirmed at the eerie quiet. "Aren't you going to ask why I'm coming?" I asked.

"No."

"Oh." I itched my neck. *Dratted hairpins.* "I just thought I might try it ... just for today."

"Very well." Beatrice kept her gaze on the road. I couldn't tell if she was pleased. She had to be pleased. I had heard her praying for me the night before, hadn't I?

We pulled up in front of the little church and climbed out of the car. Families were beginning to gather into the building. I smiled at all the mothers herding their children like chicks.

Beatrice led me into the church and settled down in the back pew. "Are you comfortable sitting here?" she asked.

The question took me by surprise. "Of course." I slid in next to her and looked around.

Beatrice smiled. "It's been said that in heaven the last shall be first."

"And who said that?"

Beatrice ducked her head, her face reddening. "For once, not me."

I smiled and looked around. It must have been a very private church, for everyone was looking at me with interest. I shifted in my seat.

The pastor was a short, balding man. He smiled easily, his face widening and his eyes crinkling. He was shaking the hand of an older woman and laughing with the man beside her. He certainly didn't look like the angry preachers I'd seen in my childhood.

Several women came to speak with Beatrice, Mrs. Wilkinson among them. She wouldn't stop gushing about Russell's wedding.

Charlie was sitting by her husband, glowing and talking to the women gathered around her. I watched her from a distance. *She never told me she'd been going to church.* I wondered if Charlie was afraid of what I'd say. Scared that I'd shut her out, like I did to everyone else. The thought that I was the kind of person my best friend might be scared of made my insides churn.

"I believe Pastor Davis is starting," Beatrice remarked sweetly, motioning for Mrs. Wilkinson to move back to her seat. Beatrice turned to beam at me.

I avoided her gaze and focused on an ant crawling across the wooden floor.

"Good morning, beloved!" Pastor Davis boomed with a surprisingly large and forceful voice.

I lowered my eyes and fiddled with my hat. *What am I doing here? I don't belong in church.*

Beatrice reached over and almost tentatively gave my hand a little squeeze. I resisted the urge to yank it away, letting it stay in her hand. I did give her a slight glare, though, to let her know I still wasn't completely happy.

"Let us turn to the book of Matthew this morning," Pastor Davis began.

I crossed my legs and watched him, my curiosity piqued. Everyone was opening their Bibles and reading the pages with care. They looked at each other with respect, and bowed their heads reverently. *So this was religion.*

I bowed my head too, although I peeked around the room. If this is what Beatrice claimed changed her life, there wasn't much to it.

I squirmed in my seat. But there was something—a sort of light in the room. I bit my lip. *I wonder what it would be like to have that light.*

May 28, 1944

Dear Sam,

Charlie and Russell's wedding went well. The reception was very nice. Russell said to send you his greetings.

There is much to do here. It seems like there's something to fix around the house or to package for the soldiers that are away. I am kept quite busy.

I send my love.

Sincerely,

Allie

I paused and stared at the sheet of paper. For someone who called herself a writer, I made a pretty lousy letter.

How would Sam feel about getting a letter from me? He wrote me every week, but I hadn't written in over a month.

My letters were short — to the point. I never embellished, never talked about my feelings.

Sam's were wonderful. His writing wasn't the best, but he always expressed so much emotion in a few words. He always asked about what I was thinking and feeling.

I crumpled up the piece of paper and started over.

Dear Sam,

I can't believe it's been nearly a year since you left. I miss you so much. June is just around the corner, and there are gorgeous roses budding everywhere. Do you remember the roses in my mother's garden? They were the most beautiful ones I've ever seen — she put so much time into them.

Charlie's wedding was so lovely I wanted to cry. It felt so strange to see sassy little Charlie all grown up and dressed in white. She had lilies for her bouquet and beautiful flowers everywhere, but Russell's allergies didn't bother him at all! (For which we were all very grateful.)

I went to church with Beatrice yesterday. I don't know what ever possessed me to go, but it wasn't awful. I wish I had a Bible so I could see if the things Pastor Davis said were true. I wish you were here so I could ask questions without being embarrassed. I haven't got a Bible, so maybe I wouldn't be able to understand it anyway.

I miss Mama.

I stopped suddenly. Why had I written *that*? Sam wouldn't want to hear about Mama.

But he knew her too. I bit my lip. Maybe he wouldn't mind a few sentences. I continued writing.

I miss Mama. She always knew the right thing to say. I've often heard people talking about how wise men give good advice, but I don't think anyone knows what to say exactly like a mother. I try to listen to Beatrice, but every time I start to think maybe she's right, a little voice pops into my head reminding me that she'll never be my mother and she'll never know the right thing to say. And so I push her away.

I hope you don't think I mean to push people away. I don't know when it started. Maybe when

Mama died. But it comes so naturally now—like breathing. I want to let people in ... I want to open up to you...

Perhaps this is just nonsense. Maybe I won't even send you this letter. Strength is important to me. I want you to think I'm strong, because I'm not.

I love you. I truly do miss you, and think of you every day.

Love,

Allie

I looked at the new letter. I sounded so weak and vulnerable—like a love-starved fool.

I sighed and folded up the letter, placing it in an envelope. Sam would understand. He knew me like no one else.

I placed the envelope on my nightstand and crawled into bed.

Where can I find a Bible? I wondered if Beatrice would notice if I took one of hers from the bookshelf.

I curled up my knees and sighed. *What's the matter with me lately?*

* * * * *

I pulled into the parking lot and looked up at Goodey's. The diner was closed, but there were still a few lights on. *Maybe Irene is still inside.*

I grabbed my keys and climbed out of the car. My heels clacked on the dark cement. I unlocked the front door and looked around. "Irene?"

A light was on in the back room. *Why would she be doing inventory at this hour?* I knocked lightly on the door before pushing it open. "Irene, I thought you said you were coming for ..." I trailed off and stood, unmoving, in the doorway.

Irene was sitting behind her desk, collapsed in a pile of tears. Her head was buried in the desk, her shoulders shaking.

"Irene?"

She looked up and sniffled. Mascara ran down her cheeks. "Allie?" She blinked at me. A letter lay discarded on the desk, crumpled and soaked.

"Is something wrong?" I ran forward and knelt at her feet. "Is it Daniel?"

Irene frowned. "What are you doing here?"

"You were supposed to meet us for supper at Beatrice's two hours ago," I said gently. "Do you remember?"

Irene sniffled. "Oh, yeah."

I looked around. *Nothing much out of the ordinary.* "What's the matter?"

Irene pointed at the letter and shrugged. "I'm sorry. I just ... I just got depressed."

"What's in the letter?"

"It's from Daniel." Irene turned back to her desk and picked up the letter. "It's just a normal letter. I don't know what I'm so emotional about." Her eyes skimmed the lines. "He talks about his new friends and what he's been reading and thinking. And he signs it 'Thankful, as always, for you and our little family; Daniel.'"

I blinked. "So then what's wrong?"

Irene took a deep breath before bursting into tears again.

"One of his …" She gasped for breath, wiping her eyes. "One of his military friends told him that his wife is expecting their first child. Daniel didn't mean to rub it in, I know. I know he's happy …" She covered her mouth with her hand to muffle her sobs.

I don't understand. I scooted forward and placed a hand on her leg. "What are you talking about?"

She shrugged her shoulders, her tears slowing down. "Daniel and I can't have children," she whispered. "He says that the two of us—that we are already our own little family. But sometimes …" She trailed off and stared at the ceiling. "I just really want a baby."

I bit my lip, unsure of what to say. "I had no idea. I mean, I just supposed …"

"That I didn't want children?" Irene sighed, clicking her pink fingernails against the desk. She stared down at the letter. "I want a baby more than *anything* I've ever wanted in my life."

I sat up. "So why don't you have one?" My blood began to boil. I grabbed Irene's skirt, tears stinging at my eyes. "Why didn't God give you a child?"

"I don't know." Irene burst into a fresh batch of tears.

I sat back and rocked on my heels, feeling disgusted. *It shouldn't be this way. People shouldn't feel this way.* I glared at the ceiling. *Do you hear that, God?*

Irene finally calmed down, lifting a strand of my dark hair. She turned it over in her hands and sniffed. "I ask myself that almost every day." She took a deep breath. "But I know that, for some reason, he chose not to." She shrugged, her voice cracking. "And I don't know why that is, but I know that it's for my good."

"How?" I glared at the floor. "How can wanting something good and honest and not getting it be for your own good?" I balled my hand into a fist. "Why does God keep us from being happy?" I whispered.

Irene looked down and seemed to really see me for the first time. She reached over and smoothed the hair off my hot forehead. "I don't know," she whispered. "But I will love him for it. I would love him if he gave me a child and I will love him if he doesn't." She wrapped my hair around her finger. "Sometimes God doesn't give us the answer that we want. But that's no excuse for being angry at him."

A lump formed in my throat. I pushed away and sniffled, wiping my nose on my sleeve. *It's not fair. Who else is there to blame if not God?* I swallowed my questions. Irene wouldn't give me the answers I wanted.

Irene was silent for another minute or two. Then she pushed away from the desk and blinked, rubbing her eyes. "Come on. I think I'm late for supper." She folded the letter, tucked it in her pocket, and smiled. "I've gotten somewhat hungry."

* * * * *

Try to say something nice. Just to see how it would sound. I looked across the table at Beatrice, who was quietly eating her supper. I bit my lip and stared at my plate. "This is good chicken," I said. "It's not nearly as burnt as yesterday's." I winced. Why was it that every compliment I gave had to be laced with a twinge of malice?

Beatrice smiled. "Thank you."

I studied her profile. She was so calm and peaceful, her

gently wrinkled face containing a glowing light. She grunted quietly, and put down her fork. I frowned. She seemed tired.

"Are you okay?"

Beatrice sighed. "Just a headache. I think I'll go lie down for a spell." She stood and pushed back her chair. "Allie, if Mrs. Wilkinson comes over with the books I loaned her, would you please explain that I'm napping and have her leave them in the living room?"

I nodded and began clearing the table.

"I'm going to go rest," Beatrice muttered again, moving slowly.

I washed the dishes before stealing into the parlor. There, sitting by Beatrice's chair, was her Bible.

I glanced at the stairs. Would she notice if I borrowed it?

Maybe it would be best if I took it outside, just in case she comes down. I grabbed the Bible and sneaked out the back door.

I walked barefoot along the shoreline until I was a safe distance from the house. Then I perched up on a rock and opened Beatrice's Bible. The pages were so thin and fragile. I flipped through them, reading all the different titles.

I stopped at the book of John. Slowly, I turned the pages, noticing Beatrice's handwriting was scrawled along the margins of the text. I traced the verses with my finger, stopping to study every underlined verse.

John 1:12–13 was circled. "But as many as received him, to them he gave the power to become the sons of God, even to them that believe on his name: Which were born, not of blood, nor of the will of the flesh, nor of the will of man, but of God."

Received him ... That was what the preacher had talked about on Sunday. The need to receive Jesus. He'd gone through the story of Jesus's death and resurrection, and explained the need we all have to repent of our sins and receive salvation.

I thumbed through more pages.

The next underlined passage was John 1:29. "Behold the Lamb of God, which taketh away the sin of the world."

I bit my lip and kept reading. I sat very still on the rock, studying well into the afternoon. The tide shifted and the sun began to sink into the sky, casting shadows over the pages.

I lifted the Bible up a little to see the page more clearly. John 3:3 read, "Verily, verily, I say unto thee, except a man be born again, he cannot see the kingdom of God." There was a small star next to the verse. My eyes fell to the bottom of the page, where Beatrice had scrawled *See Ezekiel 36:25 – 26.*

I flipped to the table of contents and found the book of Ezekiel. As I turned the pages, I glanced at the sky. *It's getting late* ... Beatrice would begin to worry.

I opened to Ezekiel 36:25 – 26. "Then will I sprinkle clean water upon you, and ye shall be clean: from all your filthiness, and from all your idols, will I cleanse you. A new heart also will I give you, and a new spirit will I put within you: and I will take away the stony heart out of your flesh, and I will give you an heart of flesh."

I gasped and nearly fell off the rock. My eyes rescanned the verse. A heart of stone? A heart of flesh?

Beatrice had written a short note in the margin. It was short and peaceful, like she'd had a smile on her face when it was written: *This is the reason why Christ died for me.*

I shut the Bible and closed my eyes. Had Beatrice reread this verse thinking of me? Had she prayed over this passage with the same mournful tears that she'd prayed over my actions the other night?

I stood and set the Bible on the rock, turning away, walking along the sand until my toes touched the softly lapping waves. A seagull flew over my head, headed for shore.

So Christ died for Beatrice? Does that mean he died for me too? I twisted my skirt around my finger. *Why would he do that for me? Why would he want to sacrifice his own life in order to give a new heart to me, of all people?*

I bent in the sand and stroked a damp seashell. *I don't deserve it. I'll never be able to deserve it. I've done too much wrong already. Today alone I've done too much wrong.* My head was so unclear and foggy. All these confusing thoughts about life and God and family … it was too much.

I rubbed my forehead and looked up at the sky. Dark clouds loomed in the distance. *Storms …*

"Allie!" someone shrieked. "Allie, come quick!"

I scrambled to my feet and ran toward the house, dropping the Bible. The side door was open. I bounded up the steps to Beatrice's room.

Mrs. Wilkinson was kneeling by the bedside, a look of panic on her face. She glanced up when she saw me blow into the doorway.

My heart was pounding in my ears as I surveyed the room. The curtains were drawn, and an abandoned book lay open on the floor. Beatrice was sprawled across the bed, eyes shut, one hand lying limp.

Mrs. Wilkinson squeezed Beatrice's hand. "Allie, call the doctor. She won't wake up."

Not again.

Chapter 16

Hope is the thing with feathers
That perches in the soul,
And sings the tune without the words
And never stops at all.

—Emily Dickinson

I paced back in forth in the hallway. I glanced at Beatrice's door: still shut. Irene sat in a little wooden chair, her head buried in her hands, murmuring to herself.

The minutes dragged on for what felt like centuries. The grandfather clock in the parlor rang, signaling the late hour.

"Irene," I whimpered. She looked up. "Do you think …" I cut myself off and turned to the window.

A single raindrop slid down the black glass, soon followed by dozens of little droplets pattering against the pane.

The Bible!

I jumped up in a sudden panic and flew down the stairs.

"Allie?" Irene called after me. I burst out the side door and ran toward the beach.

My heart was pounding. *How could I have been so stupid?*

Rain was falling freely by now, turning the sand into mud beneath my feet. My eyes stung from the salty wind as I raced through the darkness. *Where did I leave it?* I stopped at a big rock and saw a dark cover flapping in the wind. I lunged to grab it and ran back to the house.

I collapsed on the side porch in tears. I couldn't bear to look at the soppy Bible — Beatrice's prized possession — a bloating, ruined mess.

I buried my face in my knees and gasped for breath between my sobs, feeling the weight of my burden crushing me down.

Why can't I do anything right? Why can't I trust God? Why is it so much harder for me to love him and it's so easy for Beatrice and Irene? I clenched my fist. *Why can't my heart be melted too?*

"Why did you take away Mama?" I whispered, my voice drowned out in the pounding rain. "Why weren't you there when I needed you? Why didn't you help me?"

I hugged my knees to my chest and buried my face. My mind was whirling with more questions. *Why wasn't I there for Beatrice? Why am I never there for those I care about? I've never deserved her love ... never deserved her trust. And now I've messed up everything.*

I wasn't there when Beatrice's life was in danger ... wasn't there when Irene needed a comforter ... wasn't there when Sam needed encouragement and support. Oh, I wasn't even there when my own mother needed someone to hold her hand and whisper sweet things to her as she slipped away.

"God," I whispered, covering my face with my hands, "God,

I've been so wrong … so selfish. I've carved my own heart of stone and pushed everyone out. I've hurt those I love willingly and happily … I've found pleasure in causing others pain and suffering." I sniffled and wiped my nose on my sleeve. "And most of all, God … I've pushed you out. I've rejected you and closed up my heart for nineteen years. But you …" My voice broke. "Deep down, I know you died for me, Lord. You are more than enough." I closed my eyes and took a deep breath. "I don't know if I'm saying this the right way or not, but I'm sorry."

My chest shook. "I'm sorry and I want to change, God. Please help me change. I want you to be in control of me now. Help me to love others and show compassion to people." I paused before adding, "And please, God, be with Beatrice and please help her get better. Please."

I opened my eyes to see that the rain had weakened to a drizzle. I picked up the soggy Bible and stroked my hand over its cover.

"Allie!" Irene called. "Allie, come here!"

I jumped up and bounded up the stairs. Irene was standing by Beatrice's door, a doctor next to her.

He smiled at me and pushed up his glasses. "Are you Beatrice Lovell's daughter?"

I nodded, knowing it was now true. "Yes, I am. Is … Is she going to be okay?"

The doctor closed the door behind him and nodded. "Her body's been weak lately, and she suffered a mild heart attack." He reached out a hand to calm me. "No worries, though. It's not that bad. I checked her out and she seems okay. She should be awakening soon."

A slight moan came from Beatrice's bedroom. I glanced up, and the doctor gave me a reassuring smile. "There she is now. You may visit her if you like. Just be quick and quiet."

I looked at Irene. She seemed a bit confused at my eagerness to see Beatrice, but she nodded. "You go ahead."

I pushed Beatrice's door open slowly. She was lying on the bed, a dim lamp illuminating her tired face. "Allie?" she tried to smile, but her breathing was forced and labored. "Allie, is that you?"

I shut the door behind me and stood there, shaking. I could hear my heart pounding in my ears—partly from relief and partly from fear. "Beatrice?" I whispered. I looked down and saw the Bible still in my hand.

I brushed the sand off the cover and walked toward the bedside. Sinking onto the floor, I lifted the book to where Beatrice could see it.

She strained her eyes to see what I was holding. "Ah," she smiled, her voice strained and broken. "My Bible."

"I…" My hands shook. "I ruined it, Beatrice. I took it without asking and left it in the rain when you …" I broke off and looked at the floor, feeling overwhelmingly grieved. *Oh, I was so stupid. I never should have taken it … never should have ruined it.*

Beatrice lifted her hand. It shook as she labored to move it toward me. Slowly, she placed it on my bent head with the utmost care and gentleness. A soft light glowed in her wrinkled eyes as she stroked my dark hair.

She took a shallow breath, her chest shaking from the action, and yet her voice dropped to a motherly softness as she smiled at me. "I've always said …" She took a shaky breath. "I've always said that a sorry thief is better than a snooty saint." She cracked a small grin. "That didn't even rhyme."

And then I came undone. Bursting into tears, I buried my head in Beatrice's lap. "I'm so sorry," I sobbed, my voice muffled by the blankets. "I'm so sorry."

Beatrice stroked my hair, letting me unravel in her arms.

I lifted my head and wiped my tear-stained face. Beatrice smiled and bent her head, ready to listen to me.

"I ... I'm so, so sorry. For everything I've ever ... for all the things I've ever ..." I shook my head, choking back more tears. "I'm not making any sense, I know, but I just want to ..."

Beatrice nodded slowly and glanced at the Bible. "Did you ... read it?"

All I could do was nod. "Yes, I did. And now everything's going to be different for me, Beatrice. I have so much more to learn about God and Jesus and the Bible ... but it's okay now. Because God's forgiven me too, I just know it. And it's not because of anything I've done, because I haven't done anything good at all." I sniffled. "Except, maybe, that I've realized how wrong I am. And how much I love you."

At this, Beatrice's eyes began to water up. I squeezed her hand. "I love you, Beatrice. You're the best mother a girl could have." I smiled. "And I'm glad you're mine."

Beatrice began to shake. I reached out a hand to steady her. "I love you ... too, Allie."

I held her hand and watched her until she had dozed off again. And then I laid my head in her lap and, for the first time in weeks, drifted into a peaceful sleep.

* * * * *

The month of May passed slowly but surely. Beatrice made a fast recovery, and was back to her ladies' meetings and afternoons at the diner. For the first time, it felt like maybe we were going to be okay.

Then came June 7, 1944. The day after the Normandy Invasion in France. I can't remember how I discovered about the operation. Maybe it was the newspaper, maybe it was a telephone call.

I spent nearly the entire day on the side porch, staring at the ocean. Charlie came over, and together she, Irene, and I prayed and cried over the fallen soldiers.

Beatrice didn't say anything about it at all, except to squeeze my hand and whisper, "God is with him, Allie."

Pastor Davis held a special church service, ringing the bell one time for every soldier reported fallen. With every clang of the bell, I felt my heart stop for just a moment.

I rocked slowly on the porch and gripped my untouched lemonade. The ocean was rough and stormy, hitting the rocks by the cliff. Irene was beside me, murmuring about Daniel.

My mind couldn't even wander … I just sat in silenced stupor as my brain tried to soak in the thought of so many young men dying on foreign soil.

I slid my eyes shut and sent up a silent prayer for the safety of Sam: I hadn't gotten a letter in weeks.

My eyes opened and I saw my journal lying abandoned on the ground. I bent and picked it up, brushing off a little dirt. I opened it to a fresh page and smoothed down the paper.

June 7, 1944

The deep loss we all sense is nearly unbearable. And yet,

we must bear it. Everyone in town must live with the fact that our brothers and fathers and husbands and play-mates have fought and died ... and will not be coming home.

With every ring of the church bell, my body tenses, and I think "What if that's Sam's bell? What if that's Russell's bell? What if that's Daniel's bell?"

In some ways I'm glad I don't know who has fallen. And yet, maybe if we did it would help us to overcome our grief.

God seems to be the only one for America to turn to right now. Inside his arms is the only place where one can find comfort—or so I've quickly discovered. His words are the only source of peace for me at this time.

You know, the more I sit and think about it, the crazier I'll make myself. To sit and wonder ... it almost feels worse than to die.

I know I have to move on, but there seems to only be a small sliver of hope left to cling to. The small sliver that says, "Daniel will return to Irene. Russell will be back in the winter on furlough." The tiny shred of hope that tells me, "Sam will be home soon."

* * * * *

I flipped on the little lamp and settled down at my desk. I pulled out my little journal—expanded and rebound numerous times over the years—and opened it to the first page. A short poem composed on my eighth birthday filled the page. I smiled and turned more sheets.

Poems and stories and drawings filled the journal, each one sharing a small sliver of my heart and soul. Sketches of Mama and Daphne, stories of magical gardens, poems of the starry heavens—they all had a place in the notebook.

I looked up and saw Mama's old Dickinson volume sitting on the edge of the desk. I lifted it and turned to the first page. "The Heart Asks Pleasure First."

A lump formed in my throat. Mama loved that poem. Mama loved all of Dickinson's poems.

Mama loved my poems too.

The thought startled me.

But it's true—Mama did love my poems. I cradled the book in my hands and smiled as I remembered Mama's words: *"I want you to write and I want you to be happy."*

I set the volume of poems down and let my finger trace the wood pattern on the desk. *Am I happy?*

I searched deep down inside my chest for the answer. I wasn't expecting to be happy—I hadn't been happy in years.

And yet I knew I was happy. I was blessed. *When I write, I live.*

Sam had known it. Sam told me I had talent—potential. He had looked at me, and instead of seeing a miserable, foolish girl, he saw a budding poet.

I opened my journal again and read through the poems. To me, they were personal and simple. They expressed how I felt and why I felt it.

I closed my eyes. *God, what would you have me do with my writing? What can I do to honor you?*

My notebook fell to the floor with a bang. I jumped.

I leaned over to pick it up and froze. The memory flooded over me of Sam, picking up my journal and studying it intently. That was the day I fell in love with him, looking back. The day he looked at me, without a trace of laughter or teasing in his eyes, and told me, "You're better than you think, Alcyone Everly. And one day you'll know it."

I picked up the notebook and set it back on the desk without really seeing it. My heart felt like a load of bricks had fallen off of it.

I'll publish my poems.

My chest began to pound. A smile slowly spread over my face. *I'll publish my poems and make Mama proud.* I stroked the notebook. *I'll make Beatrice proud too. I'll let them both know how much I love them.*

Chapter 17

That I did always love,
I bring thee proof:
That till I loved
I did not love enough.

—Emily Dickinson

"Here, help me up." Charlie laughed and placed her hands on her back as she struggled to climb the stairs.

I grabbed her arm and helped her to the front door, sneaking a glance at her broad stomach. "He's ready to get out of there."

Charlie rubbed her belly. "The feeling is mutual."

I opened the front door and led her into the parlor, helping her out of her coat. "It sure is chilly out there," I commented, shutting out the cold.

"It's February." Charlie exclaimed. "It'll be spring before you know it."

I nodded and led Charlie to the parlor where she eased into

an armchair. "Ah." She glanced around and smiled. "I love the smell of your house."

"You mean the smell of dusty books and Beatrice's cleaning spray?"

"No, it smells like lemon and leather. Don't you wrinkle your nose — it's a good smell! Honest."

"The lemon is from the cleaning spray," Beatrice said, coming through the door with a tray of cookies. "How's the mother-to-be?"

Charlie grinned and took a cookie. "Fine, thank you."

"Any news from town?" Beatrice sat next to me and reached out to hold my hand. I smiled and let her massage the back of my wrist.

Charlie's face fell. "Michael Rosa was killed in action last week. Second man from town this year, and 1945 has just begun."

"Oh, that's awful." Beatrice's face grew pained. "I must write his mother and send her our condolences."

I shifted in my chair. "How is his fiancée taking the news?"

Charlie focused on the cookie in her hand. "Mary left town to stay with her cousin after she heard. She took the first available train the day after the funeral."

An awkward silence fell over us. "How's Irene?" Charlie asked.

"She's well, thank you. She's in town right now, actually, helping the ladies aide with the war effort." Beatrice's eyes were warm as she offered Charlie a cup of tea. "Daniel's been given leave, thank the Lord, and will be returning home any day now."

"Good." Charlie smiled, her chubby cheeks dimpling. "I received a letter from Russell yesterday, and he plans to come home in early March. I can't believe I haven't seen him since September." She blushed. "It's been nearly five months."

Both women glanced at me and fell silent. No one mentioned Sam. I lowered my eyes. He hadn't been sighted since Normandy. Something tore at my throat, coaxing me to cry. I fought it down. I didn't know if he was alive or dead, and I wouldn't cry until I got the final word. Until I knew for sure.

"More tea?" Beatrice asked, holding up the pot.

We talked for hours. About the war, and the home front, and how much things had changed since the summer of '43, when Russell and Sam were here. Charlie glanced at the clock and gasped. "Goodness gracious! It can't be six o' clock, can it? I've got to get home and prepare supper ..." Her face fell. "For myself. And this young one." She placed a hand on her stomach and gave me a half smile.

I stood. "I'm sorry to see you go." I helped her into her coat and walked her to the door. The wintry night wind whipped through my thin dress.

I hugged her gently, closing my eyes and trying not to cry. Charlie stood back and studied me from the doorway. Noticing my tears, she reached out to touch my arm. "Allie, what's wrong?"

I shook my head and smiled at her. "Nothing. I'm just glad to be here with you, because it feels like old times when we were kids." I wiped my eye. "You know, back when things were simple and happy."

"Things were never simple with you." Charlie frowned, searching my eyes. "But you seem ... different since you became a Christian. You seem happier despite ..." She cleared her throat. "Despite the circumstances."

"Everything changed when God found me," I whispered, giving her one last hug. "I just ... Remember what you said that day in the barn years ago? About how earthly things aren't enough? When I thought about that, God led me to himself. Now things seem so much easier to bear."

Charlie smiled. "How nice to know I had a small part in it."

I rolled my eyes and lightly punched her arm.

"Oh, and, Allie." Charlie met my eyes. "Don't give up on Sam. He'll be back, I know it."

"So do I," I said. And I meant it.

****

"Can I look now?" I tried to peek between the fingers sprawled across my face.

Beatrice laughed and slapped my arm lightly. "No." She led me into what I guessed to be the parlor. "Okay, now open them."

My eyes fluttered open and surveyed the room. But the moment they reached the corner, my whole body froze in shock.

"Beatrice," I whispered, my eyes beginning to swim. "You bought me a piano."

It was the most beautiful thing I had ever seen—a simple white piano, sitting by itself in the dark parlor corner. Beatrice had spread a woven burgundy runner over the lid and had a pile of sheet music stacked by the bench.

"I hope you know how to play something from the stack." Beatrice bit her lip. "I just went to the store and asked the woman for a handful of her most popular songs. I don't know anything about classical music—I really just trusted her opinion."

I stared at the piano in silence, not trusting myself to speak.

"I can return it, Allie." Beatrice waved her hand carelessly, though I could tell she was nervous. "If you really hate it."

I shook my head. I reached out and ran a finger across the piano lid softly, half fearing it would crumble at my touch. I looked at Beatrice, tears blinding my eyes. "You actually bought me a piano," I whispered.

Beatrice nodded.

"Where did you get the money?"

Beatrice waved her hand. "We're not that *poor*. Besides, one man's sale is another man's treasure."

With that, I folded myself onto the bench and burst into tears, sobbing onto the closed piano lid. When I looked up, Beatrice was standing by my side. "Is it okay, Allie?"

"Okay?" I wiped my face. "It's *wonderful*. I've never … I could never …" I turned a distressed face toward Beatrice. "What could I have done to deserve this?"

"Nothing." Beatrice looked confused. She sat down on the bench next to me and let me rest my head on her chest. "I just wanted to show you how much I love you."

"I love you too," I whispered into her shirt. And I did love her. I loved her so much at that moment, my chest was pained. I loved that she was good, and that she was kind. I loved her because of the fact she loved me and I loved her even more despite the fact that she loved me.

"Do you like it?" Beatrice asked, stroking my hair.

I turned toward the piano. "It's beautiful," I croaked. I looked up at Beatrice and smiled. "Thank you."

She beamed at me. "It made me happy to give it to you."

I took a deep breath and opened the heavy lid. I ran my fingers down the keys. "It makes me happy too."

*****

The house was dark and quiet. Only a single lamp was on in the parlor, shining almost directly on the new piano. I shut the lid and settled into an armchair, careful not to make too much noise and wake Beatrice upstairs.

My eyes threatened to close. I forced them open and yawned, closing the book of poetry lying on my chest.

I rubbed the faded cloth on the armchair and looked around the quiet house. All these years it had felt like a gilded prison; now it was finally beginning to feel like home.

Beatrice's crinkled Bible was sitting on the table. I leaned over and picked it up, running my hand down the water-worn spine. I flipped through the pages and sighed. Many of the words ran down the page or stuck together.

A yellow sheet near the front of the Bible caught my eye. I pulled it out gingerly. It was in surprisingly good condition—very few words were illegible.

My bare feet pattering on the wood floor when I crossed over to the lamp and held the paper to the light.

It appeared to be a list of important dates, written in Beatrice's hand. I smiled to myself and skimmed through the events.

June 3, 1888 — Beatrice Noble baptized age 10

May 10, 1896 — Beatrice Noble graduates

March 11, 1900 — Beatrice Noble and Henry Lloyd Lovell united in holy matrimony

November 7, 1903 — *Laura Alice Lovell born*

February 19, 1904 — *Laura Alice Lovell passes on to be with our Lord*

I paused, my eyes beginning to tear. Beatrice had another daughter, one who passed away as an infant? I wiped my eyes and kept reading.

May 27, 1910 — *Henry Lloyd Lovell passes on to be with our Lord*

I frowned. How could Henry have died before the birth of Irene? I skimmed a few more lines and gasped. My hand shook as I put down the paper.

July 6, 1922 — *Adoption of Irene Rosa Harding*

I collapsed in the closest chair, my knees quaking. Irene was adopted?

The room felt like it was spinning. I placed a hand on my forehead.

But Irene was the perfect child all along. She'd always called Beatrice Mom, and looked after her affectionately. Irene was her blood … her family.

The front door opened and Irene called out, "Hello? Is anyone awake?" She came into the doorway, open and friendly as she unbuttoned her coat. "Allie, did Mom already —"

I turned my tear-streaked face to her. She stopped, looking worried. "What's wrong? Is it Mom?"

"You were adopted." I hadn't meant it to sound like an accusation, but that's how it came out.

Irene stopped in the doorway, coat in hand. "Of course I was. You knew that."

"No! No, I didn't," I turned away. "No one ever thought to tell me."

Irene crossed the room and sank into the chair next to me. She reached out to touch my leg softly. "Allie, I …"

"I thought you were her daughter," I murmured. My stomach lurched. "You both deceived me into thinking *I* was the outsider."

"Allie." Irene sounded hurt. "We never tried to keep it from you. There was no deception or plot, I promise. I honestly thought you knew."

I turned and stared fiercely at her, although I knew I was acting like a child. "Then why didn't you tell me?"

"Maybe you just weren't listening."

I froze and met Irene's gaze.

She reached and tucked back a stray red hair behind her ear. "Allie, over the years you've spent a lot of time shutting us out. You tricked *yourself* into thinking you were an outsider. We've done nothing but treat you as a daughter and sister."

I leaned back and closed my eyes, my conscience smarting. "I know," I moaned, "I know. It's just … a shock." I glanced at Irene. "You were always so … *loving* and everything. I was always a little jealous of you. *I* wanted to be the real daughter, not the outsider. I thought …" I bent my head. "I thought Beatrice loved you more than me because you were a part of her."

Irene's eyes welled up. "*No*, honey." She wrapped an arm around my shoulder. "Beatrice couldn't love you more. I'm no more her daughter than you are. You saw that paper: we're both from the same situation." She squeezed my shoulder. "But even if Beatrice did give birth to me, she wouldn't love *you* any less. She's your mom too."

I buried my head in Irene's shoulder and sniffled. "Who was your real mom?"

Irene sighed. "She was a cabaret dancer from New York City. My father was a philanderer ... a rich banker with a love for pretty women. So I'm told—I never met him. My mother left me in the streets when I was about five. Beatrice adopted me two days after my sixth birthday. She's really the only mother I've ever known. My real mother ..." Irene trailed off. "All I really remember about her is that she had bright red hair. Like me." She stroked my cheek. "What about your parents?"

I pulled up my knees and leaned on Irene's arm. "My father left when I was three. It was really just me and Mama growing up. She was different ... *Special.*" I fiddled with a button on my pajamas. "She got the sickness when I was ten. Dr. Murphy said it was brain cancer."

"What was it like?"

I took a deep breath and stared at the wall. What *was* it like? It was hard to think of words to describe Mama and everything we went through that would make sense to someone who hadn't known her at all.

I could remember the good times and I could remember the painful times. Most vividly, I could remember the night she died.

I curled up my knees and rested my chin on them. "It was hard. To raise a mother."

Irene nodded and gave me a hug. "Well, you don't have to struggle anymore. You have a family: me and Mom and you. We all love each other."

I smiled. "I'm glad."

She tucked a piece of hair behind my ear and grinned. "So am I." Her voice softened. "Little sister."

Chapter 18

This is my letter to the world
That never wrote to me —
The simple News that Nature told —
With tender Majesty.

—Emily Dickinson

Beatrice gave my dark hair a final brush before standing back and admiring her work. I glanced in the mirror and smiled.

My deep brown waves had been swept up in the latest fashion, a dashing white hat pinned atop them. I was wearing a blue and white polka-dotted dress, with gorgeous pearl buttons running down the back, and white heels.

Irene smiled from the doorway. "You look beautiful."

I bent toward the mirror to apply a smudge of pink lipstick before smiling and turning to Beatrice. "I'm ready for church."

Pastor Davis greeted us at the church door, warmly shaking our hands. "You're looking particularly lovely today, Beatrice," he said with a shy smile before moving on.

I nudged Beatrice. "He seems to be quite fond of you."

Beatrice blushed and fanned herself. "Oh, there's Mrs. Wilkinson."

Mrs. Wilkinson walked over, all smiles. She twisted her hands and beamed at Beatrice. "Have you heard about the baby? Charlie delivered just yesterday." Mrs. Wilkinson asked.

I grinned. "Russell called, but didn't give many details at all. What are they going to name him?"

Mrs. Wilkinson winked. "They're going to name *her* Alcyone."

A wide smile spread over my face. "I'm flattered. I hope she ends up nothing like me," I teased. "For your sake."

"I must say, Allie." Mrs. Wilkinson raised a pointed eyebrow as she glanced over me. "You seem ... different. More confident and *happy*." She tucked her purse under her arm. "I do believe you've grown up." With one last glance at me, she smiled at Beatrice and turned to go. "Good day."

As she walked away, I smiled to myself. *Happy. I am happy.* I sent up a quick prayer of blessing for snooty old Mrs. Wilkinson. Then I tucked my arm through Beatrice's and guided the way to our pew. "This way, Mom."

* * * * *

"Where is Irene? She's more than two hours late."

I let the curtain drop back into place and leaned against the wall, chewing down a freshly filed nail.

Charlie smiled and poked at a streamer. "She'll be here in no time." Russell wrapped an arm around her shoulder, and she handed him Baby Alcyone. Charlie nestled under his arm and gave him a quick kiss. "Thanks," she murmured.

The telephone rang. Beatrice jumped up, chewing her lip. "Hello?" She lowered her voice. "Oh, I see."

Charlie was suddenly by my side, resting her chin on my shoulder. "Isn't it nice?" she whispered, wrapping an arm around my waist. "To care?"

I leaned into her shoulder and smiled, blinking back the tears behind my eyelids. "Yeah."

A new song drifted through the gramophone, the gentle voice singing, "When we're out together dancing cheek to cheek ..." I grimaced and tried to block the music from my ears. The song brought my wave of happy feelings to a sudden crash. *Sam. Sam, Sam, Sam.* The name echoed through my mind, torturing my thoughts.

Beatrice placed the telephone back on the retriever. "Well, it is getting late," she said, glancing at the clock. "Who knows, Allie. Maybe she'll be here by the time you get back!"

I wrinkled my nose. "Get back from where?"

Beatrice scratched her cheek. "You know what I always say on a night like this?"

I shot her a teasing look. "What do you always say?"

Beatrice reached over and patted my knee. "A midnight stroll breaks a lonely lull."

"What? That makes no sense at all."

Charlie shrugged. "You always walk when you're preoccupied—and don't deny it, it's written on your face plain as day. So why not walk now?"

I sighed and scooted out of the armchair. "Well, since everyone seems to want me to leave so badly ..." I looked around. "Does anyone wish to accompany me?"

241

They glanced at each other and frowned. "No," Beatrice said. "But we'll be here when you get back."

I reached for a navy-blue sweater by the door, sliding it over my bare shoulders. "You promise you'll call me the moment she gets here? We can't start eating the cake without her. Irene really wanted to be a part of Baby Alcyone's birth celebration."

Beatrice nodded.

"Okay, then." I trudged out the door, wrapping my sweater close. "I hope you're happy!" I called over my shoulder. The screen door closed with a slam. *They are happy for me. Because of me.* I placed my hand over my mouth. A soft smile spread behind my fingertips.

I stood by the oceanfront, bare feet in the sand, water lapping my toes, and closed my eyes. I swung my shoes from my fingers and tried to remember the moment. To remember the warm April breeze on my face … my toes in the sand.

But all I wanted in that moment was for Sam to be back. I just wanted this war to be over, and to be married. To have Sam be here again, and have his love wrap me up all safe and warm. I didn't want to stand at his funeral. I didn't want my heart to get buried in the ground and feel like I was losing a part of myself all over again.

The stars were just beginning to come out from hiding, the moon starting to softly shine.

I strained my mind to recall the Emily Dickinson poem from my childhood. In a clear voice, I recited to the waves, "The moon is distant from the sea, and yet with amber hands, she leads him, docile as a boy, along appointed sands."

I closed my eyes again and sent up a silent prayer. *Oh, God, I wish that …*

"Emily Dickinson," a voice said from behind me. "Impressive."

My body jolted. I whirled around, a shriek escaping my lips.

A tall man stood on top of a sand dune, looking down at me. He took a step toward me, his arms open. I squealed, my mind racing, and did the first thing that came to mind—throw my shoes at him.

He laughed and ducked. "Hey, watch it. Do you think I want to die?"

"Sam?" My eyes widened. There he was, standing in front of me. Right there on the beach. In front of me. Standing there.

My mind went over these stupid thoughts at least three times before I opened my mouth, ready to say my first words to him in two years. Instead, all that came out was a sob.

I collapsed in the sand, crying uncontrollably. Within seconds, Sam was on his knees at my side, wrapping his arms around me. "What's wrong?" he asked. "Allie, what is it?"

I shook my head, unable to look him in the eye. My hands wouldn't stop trembling. *It can't be true. I thought …* "I thought you were dead," I choked out. "Well, I mean, I didn't believe you were dead but I knew you might be. And after ten months …"

Sam stopped trying to talk and held me, rocking back and forth. He could probably imagine what it had felt like.

After awhile, the tears slowed down, and I pulled my head back to look at Sam. His face was the same; a little older maybe, but still the same Sam Carroll. The one who followed me around as a child. Who followed me to Maine as a teenager. He'd sat on my kitchen counter twice and told me that he loved me, and almost cried when I said I loved him too.

"Why didn't you tell me you were coming?" I finally whispered. "I've missed you so much."

Sam scooted back a little, but still held my hand tightly. He smiled, his face glowing in the moonlight. "I called Beatrice and asked her to send you out here. I arrived home a few minutes ago." He grimaced. "My train was a little late."

My heart was racing, my mind whirling. I climbed to my feet, pulling him up with me. "Well, at least let me look at you. I haven't looked at you in two years."

He stood to his full height and took a step back from me, squeezing my fingers a little. I could tell he was nervous. What would I think of the fully grown Sam Carroll?

To tell the truth, I was a little overwhelmed. He was several inches taller, now towering a full head above mine. His hair was a little longer, and his face a bit more worn. He looked like someone who had fought in battles and seen men die, who'd traveled the world and grown up while I sat here and waited for him. I covered my mouth and blurted out the first thought that popped into my dizzy head. "You're a *man*."

Sam laughed—a surprised snort. "Is that all you can think of?"

"I was afraid ..." I whispered, covering my mouth again. "I'm just so glad you're home."

Sam stepped forward and brushed a hair off my cheek. "I was going to go back to Tennessee. I was going to see my mother and my family and everything but ..." He smiled. "I telephoned Beatrice and asked to see you privately. I wanted it to be a surprise, so I could see the look on your face. I love it when you're surprised."

"So the others don't know about it?" *They're probably worried. They're probably ...*

Sam chuckled. "No, I'm sure Beatrice told them. I wrote her about a week ago, letting her know I was coming home."

"Oh." I felt so lightheaded and silly.

A gold star glistened on his uniform. I gasped and reached out to touch it. "How did you get this?"

Sam tightened his grip on my arms, smiling down at me. "You look beautiful, Allie. You look happy." He shook his head and chuckled. "You wouldn't believe how much joy your last letter gave me. I read it the day before ... the day before Normandy. Knowing that you loved me gave me the strength to be brave ... to prove myself worthy of you."

"What happened? I mean, you stopped writing me for ten months. People said you were probably dead."

Sam licked his lips. "I was caught in battle. I was shot in the ankle." He lifted his pants leg so I could see the wound, but it was dark and I could only make out faint bruising. "It wasn't a fatality, but I was left on the field for hours, stranded while everyone else left. I thought I would die. I remember thinking I might never see you again."

He fingered my cheek. I closed my eyes at his touch, my salty tears staining his hand.

"I wasn't captured, though. After about five hours, I dragged myself off the battlefield and found a tree to hide under. I was there for two days and a night, until some French nuns found me. I was driven into the city and cared for in a French hotel for about four months. A few surgeries in my leg and ankle, and then waiting for the skin to heal."

He let go of me just long enough to hold up his star so I could see it. "I got this seven months after Normandy, when I finally got back to the army. But I didn't deserve the medal. There were plenty of fallen soldiers that day who were more heroic than anything I've ever seen. Men who deserved twenty of these stars." He fingered the medal. "I guess the only reason I wear it is because the stars make me think of you."

"I always knew you were brave. Even before you joined the war. But now I'm proud of you. I think I'm prouder of you than of anything." I had to tilt back my head to see his face.

Sam reached out and touched my dark waves. "I've missed you," he whispered.

"I've missed you too." I lifted a hand and wiped a tear from my eye, laughing at myself. "I keep crying!" I rolled my eyes. "So much for hating sentimentality."

Sam smiled. "Good."

I gripped Sam's coat sleeve, my head all light and bubbly. "I was wrong about so many things." I laughed. "Especially God. But I'm better now."

Sam smiled. "I'm glad." He looked so happy and content — standing on the beach a celebrated war hero — and yet standing on the beach with *me*.

Sam's gaze turned tender. "Allie …" His voice lowered. "Do you think you could find it in your heart to marry me?"

I tilted my head back so I could see his whole face. "I think I could. I think I can fit a rather large amount of things in my heart, actually. It seems to increase every day now."

Sam squeezed my arm and leaned his forehead against mine.

"Allie!" I heard Beatrice shouting from the porch. "Allie, did you find your little surprise? Come and share it!"

I grinned and jumped back, picking up my shoes. I reached out and grabbed Sam's hand. "Come on. Mom wants me at home."

Sam picked up his suitcases and let out an excited laugh. I could see his twinkling eyes in the moonlight. "I suppose you have an awful lot to write in your little notebook."

I smiled. "Yes, I suppose I do."

Talk It Up!

Want free books?
First looks at the best new fiction?
Awesome exclusive merchandise?

We want to hear from you!

Give us your opinions on titles, covers, and stories.
Join the Z Street Team.

Visit zstreetteam.zondervan.com/joinnow
to sign up today!

Also—Friend us on Facebook!

www.facebook.com/goodteenreads

- Video Trailers
- Connect with your favorite authors
- Sneak peeks at new releases
- Giveaways
- Fun discussions
- And much more!